Wrestle the Mountain

Wrestle the Mountain

Phyllis Reynolds Naylor

Jacket Painting by *Paul Giovanopoulos*

 **Follett Publishing Company**
Chicago

ISBN 0 695-80181-3 Trade binding
ISBN 0 695-40181-5 Titan binding

Library of Congress Catalog Card Number: 79-121413

First Printing

For Michael

Chapter One

Jed tramped through the dry grass in the ditch, opposite the boy on the other side of the road. He watched Tommy Miles plodding along with his hands in his pockets and had a sudden impulse to yelp like a fox and get him laughing. But the scowl on Tommy's face stopped him.

"Rat!" came Tommy's voice suddenly. "You started it."

"I didn't."

"You almost broke my nose."

"Wish I had."

"Rat."

"Rat yourself."

"Skunk."

"Skunk yourself."

"Rat! Rat! Rat! Rat . . . !" Tommy's voice trailed off as he started up the hill at the fork. Jed followed the dirt road on around the bend, past Parsons' and a handful of other stores, and down to the scattered houses along Tin Creek.

Heck, it wasn't all that bad. They'd had a hundred scraps before. They weren't even mad at each other—just wrestling over a two-color pencil, that's all. It was getting sent home that rankled Tommy.

The West Virginia sun was still high and bright, and Jed wondered what he'd tell his mother about being home so early. It hadn't even occurred to him not to go. When Miss Singer stood in the doorway, her eyes hurt and her voice sharp, and said, "Go home at once— both of you!" it hadn't crossed his mind, or Tommy's either, to go anywhere else. It would have been like betraying the new teacher.

It was the end of September. The hills beyond Tin Creek were a patchwork of brown and red and yellow. The air was shot with rich earth odors—smells of muskrat castor, pines, and Winesap. The road billowed up orange dust where Jed walked. He picked up a walnut and threw it at a bull rabbit leaping through the checkerberries.

Jed could see the roof of his house through the sycamores that lined the road, and his feet slowed a bit. Even before he reached the yard, he could smell the strong odor of lye and knew that his mother was washing clothes on the porch.

As he started across the grass, her arms rose slowly out of the tub. She paused a moment, with her shoulders stooped, then let her arms slide down the washboard again.

"Why you home, Jed?"

"Teacher sent me."

"Sick?"

"Don't think so."

He came on up the steps, his father's shoes clumping loosely on his feet, passed his mother, and went inside. He got a drink of water at the pump in the kitchen and then went out on the back stoop and took the shoes off.

His mother followed him, wiping her arms on her skirt. "Stomach hurt or anything?"

"No. I'm okay."

"You ought to lie down maybe till your dad gets home."

"Naw. I'll just sit out here."

She waited a minute, then went back to her work. Jed leaned against the door frame.

Jed Jefferson Tate. The name had been carved in the wood of the back stoop two years ago and still read sharp. That was because Jed dug deep with his knife. *Samuel Harrison Tate*, his father. For five generations, the Tates had given their sons at least one president's name. Somewhere along the line there was even a Lincoln Washington Tate, he'd been told. And they'd all worked the mines—five generations.

He pulled out his pocketknife and began carving on a whistle he'd started the day before. He remembered the pillow fight he and Tommy had had last week out behind Parsons' and chuckled. It had been black as pitch, and they found those old couch cushions and began swinging them at each other in the dark. Pow! The thing about pillow fighting in the dark was that you never knew when one was coming at you. He grinned wider. He'd make this whistle for Tommy.

Jed could hear the squeal of the school bus at the fork, a few shouted good-byes, and then the slow grind of the motor as it started on up the hill past the church and the cemetery beyond. He sat listening for the sound of his sisters' voices. April Ruth came first, humming to herself, and Jed heard the thump of her books inside the front door. Then Beatrice, talking to Mother.

"Wash my dress, Ma, while the water's soapy?"

10

"For goodness sake, Bea, you'll wear out the cloth!"

"Please, Ma," Beatrice pleaded, and there was no more talk—just the rubbing of the washboard.

Jed carved some more on the whistle and wondered what Tommy was doing. Eating lard bread and swinging on his front porch, he imagined.

Now April Ruth was badgering her mother about Morgantown.

"How should I know how many schools they got, April Ruth?" came Mrs. Tate's high voice in exasperation. "That's what books is for. Go up to the parsonage and ask can you borrow the encyclopedia. What kind of paper you got to write?"

"I got to pick me a city in West Virginia and learn all about it. Where's Jed?"

"Out on the stoop."

Jed went on whittling and didn't even look up when April Ruth appeared in the doorway. He knew what she wanted.

Some people mistook Jed and April Ruth for twins. They were both tall and slim and each had large hands and big feet, more noticeable on Jed. Each had the same sand-colored hair and the same gray eyes. But April Ruth was a year older, and there were other differences, too. Jed's cheekbones stuck out prominently. His ears were small, giving him the appearance of a young fox. When he smiled, the corners of his lips turned down a little, which made him look as though he were only half happy.

"Jed," said April Ruth. "You seen the minister's new pups—Sukey's litter?"

"No."

"You ought to go while they're still cute—white paws like Sukey's, every one of 'em."

"Naw," said Jed, and went on working.

April Ruth sat down on the stoop, her long legs stretched out before her.

"Give you half a banana if you go to the parsonage and bring me back the *M* book."

"Where'd you get the banana?"

"I don't have one yet, but Ma said maybe she'd get some at the store tomorrow. I'll give you half mine."

"Don't want it. Get your own book."

"Whole banana?"

"Nope."

"Lazy!" April Ruth got up and clattered inside in disgust.

Jed laughed to himself.

Big Tate got home fifteen minutes after the sun had sunk behind the mountains. Evening

12

came early in this cavern between the hills. Jed sat on the stoop watching the sun disappearing, until finally the reds and golds and browns of the distant trees gave way to gray, and the mountain looming up behind the house turned into the familiar black giant that Jed knew so well. Outlined against the late afternoon sky, the mountain—which began just beyond Tin Creek—looked like his father's head and shoulders when he was dozing off at the table, his big arms resting on his newspaper, and his head tipping lower and lower. There were ridges on one side of the mountain that formed his nose and lips and chin, and a point on the other that looked like the small tuft of hair at the nape of his neck.

When the mountain began to look like his father's head, Jed knew it was almost time for Big Tate to get home. He'd listen for the whistle at the mine which meant the day crews were coming up. Not long after that, he'd hear his father calling him outside the kitchen window, and he'd go work the pump handle up and down, forcing water through the hose and out the kitchen window in a special shower Big Tate had rigged up for warm weather.

When the weather was cold—November or so—Big Tate came into the kitchen and stripped to the waist. Then he got down on his hands and knees and leaned over a washtub full of hot water, lathering his hair and shoulders and arms.

"Jed?"

Jed quickly put his knife back in his pocket and ran into the kitchen. His father was looking at him through the window.

"Let 'er go!"

Jed pushed the end of the hose onto the pump spout and pumped as hard as he could. The gurgle of the water grew louder as it came bubbling up the pump and through the hose to the outside. Jed shivered involuntarily as he heard his father grunt, the way he always did when the cold water hit his body.

Thirty-seven, thirty-eight, thirty-nine, Jed was counting to himself. Forty. That's how many pumps it usually took before his father yelled, "Enough!" He picked up the towel and took it around to the makeshift shower stall.

In the evening dusk, his father's body stood out shiny and clean against the dark of the house. His work clothes lay in a heap on the ground and would stay there until Jed's mother picked them up later and put them in a tub to soak until washday. There was a patch of gray hair in the center of his father's head, and Jed could never see it until the coal dust had been washed off. Then, like a patch of new grass, the gray showed up stiff and high.

14

Like most miners, Big Tate had marks on his cheekbones and one ear, because these were the parts of the face which stuck out and were hit when small rocks fell. Miner's tattoo the marks were called.

"Ahhhhh," said Big Tate, vigorously rubbing his back with the edge of the towel, making red stripes in the brown flesh. "Ahhhhhh," as he rubbed the towel hard over the back of his neck. And then finally, "Ahhhhhh!" of a different sort, which meant he was through. He looked at his son as he wiped his face. "How's the new teacher?"

"Okay."

"She teachin' you numbers and spellin', ain't she? Not just crayon pictures . . ."

"Sure. She's a good teacher."

"Hope you get on, then."

There was pork with beans at supper and big hunks of brown bread, made fresh that morning.

"I reckon it's ready," Lona Tate said, once it was on the table, and for the first part of the meal, no one talked much, attending to the business of eating. Big Tate covered his bread with a layer of cooked cabbage and ate rapidly, wiping his plate each time with the bread. It was a good meal, with rice pudding, too, and there were raisins!

"Daddy, what's the population of Morgan-town?" April Ruth asked.

"She's writin' a paper for school, and her legs are too soft to walk up the hill and borrow a book from the parsonage," Mrs. Tate said, frowning at her youngest daughter.

"I did so, Ma, but the minister weren't home. You wouldn't want me to walk on in and take it, would you?" She turned back to her father. "Don't you know the population, Daddy?"

Big Tate cocked his head, a trace of a grin on his face. "Well, I don't usually carry figures around in my head, gal. But guessin', I'd say maybe twenty—twenty-five thousand. How's that sound?"

"You'd better check it, April," Beatrice warned. "I had Mrs. Barnes a couple years ago, and you've got to be right."

Big Tate turned to Beatrice. "What's this I hear 'bout you thinkin' on quittin' school, Bea?"

"All I said was I'm thinkin'. I haven't made up my mind certain."

"Well, you think a long time, little gal, 'cause it's a sad thing to have a school there and not use it. The way it costs, now, it's a wonder any of you get to go. They change the books too regular, for one thing." He ate

16

silently a moment, thinking over what he'd said. "You're fixin' to marry, I suppose. . . ."

Bea said nothing, but the determined way she jabbed at her food said maybe. Beatrice was shorter than either Jed or April Ruth and already had the full figure of a grown woman, though her legs were spindly. She was pretty in a dull sort of way, but she moved slowly, as though looking at life through sleepy eyes, Jed thought. Maybe she should get married. Maybe it would hurry her up.

There were footsteps on the porch and a sharp banging on the front door.

Jed could see the door from where he sat, and waited—stuffing his mouth with rice pudding—while his mother answered. His jaws stopped moving as the door swung open, for there stood Tommy Miles with his father.

"Evenin'," said Mother, opening the door wider. "Won'cha come in?"

"Not exactly a callin' visit," replied Tommy's father, Sedge Miles, without moving. Jed could see that he had one big hand on the back of Tommy's neck.

"What's the matter then?" asked Mother, and everyone at the table grew quiet, listening. Father, especially, sat motionless, listening—his eyes hard and unblinking.

"I heard our boys was fightin' at the school

today and got sent home by the teacher. Hasn't never happened before to Tommy, gettin' sent home, and I'm not sayin' who's to blame. But if it's a fight they're wantin', then let 'em have it out and done with. I brung Tommy over to finish it up proper out here in the yard, if you're willin'."

Big Tate sprang from the table and grabbed Jed's arm as he moved, striding swiftly to the front door and dragging Jed with him.

"I heard that," he said, and there was no kindness in his eyes for the man on the porch. He looked down at his son. "This true, Jed?"

The rice pudding slid down Jed's throat and landed with a thud in his stomach. He wiped one arm across his mouth. "Yes."

Big Tate pulled Jed out on the porch with him. "Okay," he said, "let 'em fight it out."

The two boys faced each other on the porch. Out of the corner of his eyes, Jed could see his mother and sisters watching from the window. Sedge Miles stood on one side of the boys and Samuel Tate on the other. Even in the darkness, Jed could see Tommy's teeth chattering and his face as white as the day he threw up in church.

"You started it," Tommy began hesitantly. "You grabbed my pencil. . . ."

Jed licked his dry lips. "You took my

apple out of my sack. I was just gettin' even."

"You ain't here for a debatin' match," said Sedge. "Get out there on the grass and lay into each other, if that's what you were so keen on doin' at school."

Jed walked down the steps beside Tommy. They went out into the middle of the yard, where it was darker still. Then they stood with their eyes on the ground, their shoulders hunched up, hands in their pockets.

"What'cha waitin' for?" called Sedge, trying to see through the shadows. "Go on."

Tommy drew up his fist and took a tentative poke at Jed's shoulder. Jed hit Tommy in the chest. Then they both stood still.

"Come on!" yelled Sedge. "Fight, doggone it!"

"They don't need a cheerin' section." Big Tate's voice was cold. "Let 'em settle it themselves."

Tommy hit Jed again. Jed grabbed Tommy's arm and swung him around, knocking him down. He fell on top of him and pinned his arms to the grass.

"You moron," Jed whispered. "Why'd you tell your pa?"

"I didn't. Ma did."

"What we supposed to do out here?"

"Kill each other, I reckon."

"If you guys are gonna fight, *fight!*" roared Sedge. "If you wanna have a little discussion, I'll bring ya some tea!"

"You keep out of it, Sedge," Big Tate said tersely.

"He's my kid, and I won't have him made into a pansy," Sedge retorted. "You kids don't speed it up, I'll come out and land a few myself."

"He means it," Tommy whispered.

An owl screeched from the sycamore trees, and a stray hen clucked somewhere around the porch, looking for a place to roost.

Tommy rolled over suddenly, knocking Jed off, and jumped to his feet. He put up his fists the way boxers do and went dancing around and around, taking little jabs now and then. Jed watched, wide-eyed. Something about it wasn't right. Tommy was on his tiptoes, or something, and his legs were too stiff. He looked like a heavyweight trying to do a polka. Jed wanted to howl with laughter, but didn't dare. Now Tommy was taking little swipes at his stomach.

"Throw in your left! Throw in your left!" Sedge yelled from the porch, exasperation in his voice.

The boys went into a clinch. Jed grabbed Tommy's shoulders, and they went reeling around the yard together.

20

"My God!" said Sedge. "Now they're waltzin'!"

"I got an idea," Tommy whispered. "Let's knock each other out."

"How?"

"Back up a couple feet, and we'll both lunge together. You hit me with your right and I'll hit you with mine, and make it look real bad."

They each backed up and hunched their shoulders. In the darkness, Tommy looked like a gorilla stalking out of the bushes. With fists poised, they went rushing at each other, and the impact sent them sprawling.

Jed lay still. The owl screeched again.

"Now what!" said Sedge.

A low moan shattered the stillness and came from the spot where Tommy lay. Jed's flesh crept. Again Tommy moaned, and this time he sounded suspiciously like he had on Halloween.

Big Tate was bending over Jed. "Jed, you hurt?"

Jed didn't answer.

Big Tate took Jed's arms and lifted him up. Jed produced a low moan of his own.

"Can you walk?" asked his father.

"I . . . I think so."

"Go on in the house."

Slowly Jed limped over the yard. He

passed Tommy who was being hoisted to his feet by Sedge. Their eyes met as Jed passed, and Tommy moaned again for good measure.

"They should be in the ring!" Sedge was saying. "They should be in the ring! Only two fighters in West Virginia can knock each other out. Hell!"

Big Tate didn't answer. He went up on the porch and stood with his arms at his sides until Sedge and Tommy got out to the road. Jed went in and crawled onto his cot with his clothes on. He pulled the blanket up under his chin, his chest heaving with silent, explosive laughter.

Big Tate came into the front room. The laughing stopped. Jed lay absolutely still, his eyes wide open, watching his father come. For a moment, Big Tate stood by the cot, looking down at Jed. Then, without a word, he shook his head and walked back to the table in the kitchen.

Jed closed his eyes and turned over, smiling. Tomorrow he'd give the whistle to Tommy.

Chapter Two

It had not been forgotten in the morning. When Jed awoke to the clink of coals in the stove next to his cot, he could hear his mother talking in the kitchen. And when he lifted his ear from the blanket, he could make out what she was saying.

"I don't care if it was the *worst* kind of fightin'! She shouldn't have sent him home. What's happened to the old ways of punishin'? It's as though she don't want to touch 'em—as though she's turnin' 'em out, like she's washin' her hands of 'em."

"It's what comes of bringin' a teacher in from the outside," said Big Tate, and Jed could hear the clank of his fork on the wooden table. "Maybe it's the Ohio way of doin' things, but it won't go here. She'll have half the school comin' home afternoons. She can't handle 'em, we ought to get someone who can."

Jed closed his eyes. That's what he was afraid they'd say. Pretty soon Uncle Caully and Aunt Etta would be saying it too, and then the Mileses and the Parsons and the Hardys. Once they decided the teacher wouldn't work out, they'd find fault with everything she did. And when summer came, she'd leave Tin Creek like the other teachers before her, never to come back.

It didn't work talking of getting someone from your own people. Those who went to the colleges never seemed to come back. And there wasn't anybody here who had enough schooling to be a teacher.

April Ruth came out of the smaller bedroom and dumped her clothes on the floor in front of the stove. "Turn your head," she ordered, and Jed rolled over, facing the wall, while April Ruth and then Bea dressed in the warmth of the coal stove. It was the second morning they'd had heat in Septem-

24

ber. That meant it was a cold winter coming up.

By the time the girls were ready for breakfast, Big Tate was on his second cup of coffee, which he always brought into the front room, and drank while he listened to the morning news on the radio. That was Jed's signal to get up.

But this morning the radio stayed quiet. Big Tate set his thick mug down on the floor beside his chair and set to work putting new laces in his boots.

"What kind of fightin' was it you done at school yesterday, Jed?"

Jed rolled over slowly. "Just the playin' kind. Weren't even mad."

"The teacher don't like you, then—nor Tommy, neither. That it?"

"No. That's not it. She's the same to all of us."

"She don't like any of you?"

"Sure she does. She likes us all. She's okay."

Big Tate reached down and picked up the other boot. "Well, do your fightin' out of school, here on. And next time you pick a fight with the Miles boy . . ." he hesitated a moment, deftly threading the black lace through the eyes of the boot, ". . . *especially* the Miles boy . . . finish it off proper."

It had turned colder overnight, and Jed wore his gray jacket to school. The road sloped gently upward as it passed Parsons' and the nickel-and-dime. But once it divided at the fork, where the "bosses' row" houses perched haughtily on its left path, the right path continued upward, climbing sharply on up, looking down on the church and parsonage nestled in the hollow, until it reached another road, once gravel, but now mostly dirt. Turning left, one would eventually reach the blacktop road that took the older boys and girls to high school. But Jed turned right toward the old field schoolhouse, where the road ended eventually at Mine Number 7 and the slag pile beyond.

Halfway up the hill, Jed met Jolly Parsons and wished he hadn't. Anybody walked by the store, Jolly never missed him. She'd undoubtedly know something about last night. For the daughter of a grocer, Jolly was unusually skinny, and perhaps this was why she hardly seemed like a girl at all. Whenever Jed thought about her, which wasn't often, he remembered a wide grin mounted on toothpick legs, with long black straight hair almost to the waist.

"Hurry up," she called, shivering. "Tommy already passed."

Jed came up beside her without answering, and they hurried on, bending their heads before the wind that blew the red rust in their eyes.

"Yesterday sure turned into something, didn't it?" Jolly said, half-delightedly, her long hair blowing wildly about her face. "Saw Tommy and his pa heading down toward your place last night. You get thrashed?"

"Naw. What's it to you?" Jed scowled as he bucked the wind. Why was it that girls always like to get something started—something they could watch?

Miss Singer's bell sounded as they reached the rim of the hill, and Jed and Jolly ran all the way, squeezing in the door at the end of the line.

Tommy was in the hall getting a drink from the pail and dipper. He grinned as Jed knew he would. "We oughta be in the movies," he said.

Jed laughed and slipped the whistle in his hand. "Skunk."

Tommy looked down. "Hey, Jed! Thanks!"

Miss Singer was sorting through a pile of arithmetic papers, quieting the younger children who were in the first rows. She wore a green skirt and sweater, and her hair was pulled back from her face and tied with a big

bow of green yarn. She looked different today somehow—more reserved, perhaps, and
controlled.

All through the morning, she led the reading recitation and multiplication drill with
businesslike efficiency, studiously avoiding
Jed's or Tommy's eyes. Her young face, halfway between pretty and plain, was set in a fixed
expression, and every so often she pushed back
her reddish blond hair in an attitude of relaxed
calm.

But Jed could hear the false cheerfulness
in her voice, and he hated it. He hated that she
had to try so hard. He hated that she was dis-
liking her job already. If she quit at Christmas,
like the teacher did last year, there would be
another succession of substitutes from December to June, and maybe even Uncle Caully
would have to substitute again. The only things
Uncle Caully knew were about one-hundred
verses of *John Henry* and the history of the
United Mine Workers of America in West Virginia. And you couldn't get very far on that.
What if Jed got to junior high next year and
they wouldn't take him? What if he couldn't
pass the tests and had to come back and do
sixth all over again? April Ruth had got in by
the skin of her teeth. It could happen . . .

At recess, Miss Singer stopped Tommy and

Jed on their way outdoors. When the room was empty, she said, "I overheard some of the children talking yesterday, and I guess I was wrong in sending you home. They misunderstood how I meant it, and they've been saying I don't like you. That's not the case, of course. I won't send you home again."

"Yes, ma'am," said Jed.

They waited and she waited, but nobody knew what else to say.

"I've . . . never switched a child in my life, though, and I'll not start now," said Miss Singer, suddenly busying herself with some chalk in the tray. "If you can't behave in the classroom, I'll think of some other way to discipline you."

"Yes, ma'am," said Tommy.

They went outside and stepped over the girls who sat crowded on the school steps singing church hymns. That's all they ever did at recess—that or skip rope. "A Little Talk With Jesus Makes It Right," they were singing, and when they finished that one, somebody started "Revive Us Again." A Sunday school teacher came around in a jeep two Sundays a month and picked up all the kids from ten miles around who wanted to come to church. The girls always went because they liked to sing.

Jed and Tommy walked as far away from

the girls as they could go without getting away from the building and into the path of the wind which was whipping across the bare playground.

"You think she's fixin' to leave, Jed?" Tommy asked.

"Can't hardly tell," Jed mused. "I know one thing though—I'm not fightin' you no more in the schoolhouse. I'll bust you goin' home from school, maybe, but not so's she can see. . . ."

They stood there hunched up against the wind, remembering the night before, and started laughing. The girls on the steps thought they were laughing at them and sang even louder.

It was just after lunch, when Miss Singer had started reading from a biography of Benjamin Franklin, that Uncle Caully appeared in the doorway. He had his work clothes on and looked as though he'd been painting someone's kitchen, because he had specks of pink and green paint on his trousers and held a gray work cap in his hands.

Caully was the oldest of the Tate boys, and Samuel Tate—Jed's father—was the youngest, and there was almost twenty years difference between their ages. Where Big Tate had black hair that was graying at the temples, Uncle

Caully's hair was completely gray, and he had a Santa Claus mustache and beard which reached all the way down to the second button on his shirt. He stood there at the door, leaning on his good leg and waiting to get the teacher's attention.

Miss Singer sensed the distraction and looked up. "Yes?"

"Pardon, ma'am, but I'm Jed Tate's uncle, and his ma sent me to fetch 'im. Their pig's got loose. Just went through Parsons' store, makin' a terrible mess. It'll take two, three young folk to catch it. . . ." He pushed up the silver-rimmed glasses on his nose and waited.

Miss Singer stared at Uncle Caully. "Do you mean that I'm to excuse some of my pupils to catch a pig?"

"Yes, ma'am," said Uncle Caully graciously.

Miss Singer stood motionless, debating with herself. "The children are in the middle of a lesson," she said, ignoring the dozen of hands waving before her, begging to be chosen. "Is there no one else who can catch it?"

"Men are in the mines, ma'am, and the ladies ain't as quick as they used to be."

Somehow, the way he said it brought a burst of laughter from the children, but Miss Singer bit her lip. "All right," she said. "Jed, you may go, and Tommy, you may help him."

Jolly Parsons leaped up. "And me, ma'am, 'cause if it's in our store, I'll know best how to catch it."

Miss Singer smiled faintly. "All right—the three of you, then. I'll expect you back as soon as the pig is caught."

The three were halfway down the road, leaving Uncle Caully hobbling far behind, before Jed let out a whoop and leaped down into the ditch, spinning like a top. There should be more pigs loose in September! If only Jolly hadn't come, it would be perfect.

"Hey, Jolly," he said. "What makes you think you can catch a pig?"

Tommy grinned. "She's gonna scare it stock still. It'll see Jolly comin' and think it's a walkin' stick."

Jolly smiled ruefully but continued along beside them.

"Maybe she's gonna ride its back," said Jed. "Lasso it with her hair ribbon."

"I know more'n you do about pigs," said Jolly. "We used to have a whole lot of pigs before Pa bought the store. Why, we used to have pork near every Sunday. . . ."

That reminded Jed of what his father was saving the pig for, and he started to run. The stupid animal had probably knocked down the makeshift fence in the backyard. Mother had said the yard was no place for a pig, but Big Tate wanted to keep it till December and have roast pork for Christmas dinner.

" 'Twill be a hog by then," Uncle Caully had told them. "You put that thing on the table Christmas, with an apple in its mouth, and there won't be room for nobody to sit down."

"Then we'll cure it and have enough meat to last the winter," Father had said. When somebody gave you a pig, you just didn't turn it down, no matter how much feed it took to fatten it up or how much trouble to keep it penned. If Jed didn't catch that pig, there wouldn't be any Christmas dinner at all—not the way the money was going.

As they neared the stores, Jolly's mother came out of the grocery and waved them on. She was a tall, thin woman, twice as tall as Jolly and just as thin.

"Jed Tate, that pig of yours knocked down a jug of vinegar and ran right through a crock of potato salad," she called. "It shied through the apple bin and out the back door 'fore I could take the yardstick to 'er. You better hurry before she reaches the county road."

Behind the store, a bed of white and yellow chrysanthemums lay flattened as though the tire of a truck had run through them. Beyond that, a row of hollyhocks were parted in the middle. The pig was halfway down the creek, delighted with its new freedom.

"Soo-wee! Soo-wee!" Jed called, but the pig's short legs went all the faster. Every time the pig stopped and Jed and Tommy had almost reached her, she'd dart forward again with a jerk of her head and go shooting off down the bank, the boys screaming behind her. As she crossed the Tates' yard, she paused momentarily to inspect the fallen fence and then dashed on, a strange pig-smile on her face.

Further down the creek, the pig slowed again and began rooting about in a pile of beet tops which someone had thrown away. It was only a few feet from the swinging footbridge that led to the potato fields across Tin Creek, right at the base of the mountain.

"You and Jolly stay on this side and see if you can get the pig to go out on the bridge," Jed whispered. "I'm goin' across and come up the bridge on the other side. We'll trap her in the middle."

Jed leaped across the creek at the shallow point and ran along the bank till he got to the bridge. Then he crouched low and waited.

Tommy and Jolly began edging closer and

closer toward the pig, who had her snout buried in the beet tops. Reluctant to leave her lunch, the pig began moving away with her hind feet, keeping her snout in one place, until the two were upon her, and the only way out was across the swinging bridge. The pig gave a loud grunt, scurried up on the bridge, and took a few steps.

It was the first time the pig had been on a bridge, swinging or not. She was not used to the look of water below, and suddenly she gave an ear-splitting squeal.

"Get 'er, Tommy!" Jed yelled, running toward them across the swaying bridge.

"I got 'er!" Tommy yelled, throwing himself on the pig.

"I got 'er!" Jolly yelled, throwing herself on Tommy.

But nobody had the pig. Six hands reached out to grab her, six hands touched her, but the pig—like a slithering sausage—gave another terrified squeal, nipped Tommy's arm, leaped on Jolly's back, and went running back over the bridge and on along the bank toward Uncle Caully's house and the new road.

"You stupid girl!" Tommy yelled, looking for someone to blame. "If you hadn't jumped on my back, I would have had her!"

But it was no time to bawl out Jolly. Jed wanted that pig so badly for Christmas dinner he could taste it, three months away.

"Okay, Jolly," he said. "You tell us. How do you catch a pig?"

Jolly's nose twitched, and the dimple in her left cheek grew deeper. "You won't listen."

"Yes we will, Jolly. We'll do whatever you say."

"Okay. You got to sweet-talk her."

"Got to what?"

"Sweet-talk her. You got to call her pretty names in a gentling voice, like you rock a baby to sleep."

"Aw," said Tommy. "That won't work."

Jolly shrugged. "See? I said you wouldn't listen!"

"Look, Tommy," Jed said. "If that's the way to catch a pig, we got to do it. You call 'er, Jolly."

"Won't do no good for me to sweet-talk her," Jolly insisted. "She's a girl-pig and you're fellas. That's the difference."

"Come on, Tommy," Jed said, walking slowly after the trotting pig. "You got to help." He put his hands to his mouth. "Here, sugar baby! Here, honey! C'mon, pretty girl!"

"Here, sugar! Here, sweetheart!" yelled Tommy. "Is that the way, Jolly?"

36

Jolly nodded and hung back while the boys went after the pig—on down the hill toward the new road, where a coal truck could kill a pig instantly if it were silly enough to venture out. The pig began to veer right, however, avoiding the new road ahead. Instead, it ran along the side of Uncle Caully's house, crossed the dirt road, and began running over to the small postal station that stood on the corner of Jed's dirt road and the new county highway.

There was a small flag waving from the white concrete station, and Jed hoped that Aunt Etta, who was postmistress of the village, would not rush out suddenly and frighten the pig again.

"C'mon, beautiful sweetie!" he yelled. "C'mon, pretty lady! Here, little piggy! C'mon!"

By now the pig had broken into a gallop, and it began to look as though she was going to leap right over the steps of the postal station and head right out for the highway. The boys broke into a run, and their voices grew louder and more frantic.

"Here, baby sweetheart! Here, lovely darlin'. Here, beautiful honey!" Jed yelled, thinking of all the sweet talk he ever knew.

Suddenly the door of the postal station opened, and Aunt Etta stepped out, a big-shouldered woman with gray, curly hair and round, pink cheeks that sagged under the weight of their fifty years. She couldn't believe her ears. Quickly she darted inside and came back with an armload of empty mailbags. As the pig ran up, with the boys screeching honeyed phrases behind her, Aunt Etta threw the sacks on the pig and stopped her just long enough for Jed and Tommy to dive together and grab her, holding her fast.

Aunt Etta stood there on the steps, surveying the tangle of boys and pig.

"Well," she said at last, "now that you got her, which of you boys is goin' to marry her?"

"Marry her?" squawked Jed.

"With all that sweet talk oozin' around, I figure she must be some pig!" said Aunt Etta. "Why, you boys sound like you're plumb loco. No wonder the poor thing was runnin' so fast." She came down off the porch, opened a large mail sack, and they all worked to shove the pig in, tying the sack fast again with only the pig's head sticking out.

Jed stood up. "We were just tryin' to catch her," he said, his face burning. "Jolly said it was the way to catch a she-pig. . . ." He glanced up the hill. Jolly was standing twenty yards back, leaning against a tree and holding her sides, laughing up a fit.

38

"Somebody pulled your leg good," said Aunt Etta, smiling too. "Sweet-talkin' a pig! Why, you boys are somethin' else!"

"That Jolly!" yelled Tommy, struggling to his feet and starting up the hill after her, but Jolly was already on her way back to school, and skinny or not, her legs were second to none. In moments, she had disappeared around the bend.

When Jed and Tommy reached the school, Jolly was already in her seat and Miss Singer was just closing the biography of Benjamin Franklin.

"I'm sorry it took you so long," she said as Jed sat down. "I'll want the three of you to read this book on your own time. There will be test questions on it later." She slid the book back on the shelf and hesitated a moment. Her brown eyes looked up. "Did you catch the pig?" she asked, smiling faintly.

"Yes, ma'am," said Jed.

She smiled big now. "Good."

She was trying, really trying, Jed decided as the afternoon wore on and science gave way to geography and finally to art and the West Virginia hills.

"The country is so beautiful up here. It's positively breathtaking from this window,"

Miss Singer said, passing out large sheets of white paper. "No matter how long we look at that mountain, we all see it a little differently. I'll be interested in how each of you paints it."

Jed wondered if she knew about the slag pile back of the mine at the foot of the mountain—about how it had oozed over onto the Barlows' property up there, covering the well and the spring and a fruit basement. He wondered if she knew how they were ripping out coal from that mountain, while the silt washed down the mountainside, filling the creek bed, and causing floods in Tin Creek that didn't use to be. He wondered if she knew that sulfur entered the streams, and how you couldn't go swimming anymore in Tin Creek because the acid burned your eyes. But Miss Singer said the mountain was beautiful, so everyone got ready to paint it.

When the teacher finally got the lids off the paint jars, however, she discovered that the paint was old and dried up, and everyone had to use crayons instead, which wasn't nearly so pretty. The children set about listlessly drawing big black or green humps on their paper, calling it "mountain," ignoring the fall colors. Miss Singer sensed their lack of enthusiasm and blamed it on the paint. On top of that, a bee got into the room, upsetting the first graders in the front row. In their efforts to get away, they trampled on their drawings, making them uglier still.

Silently, Miss Singer picked up the dusty papers as the clock struck three, and the children trooped out the door for home. Jed hung back. He wanted to say something to her, something nice—even thank her for letting him go after the pig. At that moment, however, the three last pupils in the hallway started to leave.

A gust of air swept the door from their hands, banging it hard against the wall, and the mountain wind rushed into the room, blowing the spelling papers into a whirlpool above the desk and sending the rest of the crayon pictures flying against the blackboard and scooting across the dirty floor.

Miss Singer stared at the sudden mess, and her eyes filled to the brim as though she could not stand this one more thing. The door slammed again and the children were gone, and only Jed had seen her turn quickly toward the window to hide her face.

"I'll get them," he said hurriedly, not knowing what else to say to a teacher who was obviously crying. He moved rapidly about the room collecting the drawings. "It's only the ones on the bottom got dirty."

Miss Singer said, "Thank you," with her

back still to him, and pretended that she was fixing the pencil sharpener on the window sill.

Jed put the papers on her desk again. Then he waited a moment, and when she still didn't turn around, he got his jacket, opened and closed the door carefully, and started home.

I'll make her a paperweight, he decided, walking along with his collar turned up.

But he knew what that meant. It meant showing something to Miss Singer he'd never shown to anybody else, not even Tommy. It meant reaching into the front closet at home and taking out something that no one, not even Mother, knew was there. It meant giving away a little bit of a secret that Jed had kept inside him for over a year. But he was going to do it.

He was so busy creating the paperweight in his mind that he didn't even think of the pig again till he got home.

Chapter Three

The reason Jed remembered the pig was because it was still tied up in a mail sack on the
front porch, with only its head sticking out.
Uncle Caully had hauled it up from the postal
station and left it there for Big Tate to reckon
with when he got home.

Jed went inside. He buttered a piece of
cold corn bread and ate it between bites of an
apple, watching his mother work.

Mrs. Tate dumped a pan of dough onto her
floured board and began to punch it down.
"We're gonna have to sell the pig, Jed. That's

all there is to it. The stove broke down again this mornin', and this time Caully says he can't fix it. I got to bake my bread at Etta's. We can get by till June without the refrigerator workin', but we got to have us a stove, and it'll cost sixty, seventy dollars, maybe, to get one that's workin' good." She tried to laugh it off, the wrinkles deepening in her cheeks. "No use savin' a pig for Christmas if there's no oven to roast it in."

Jed liked the way she looked when she smiled. Lona Tate was considerably younger than her husband, and her long, honey-blond hair was still pretty, the way it was when Big Tate married her seventeen years before. But the wrinkles in her face were deepening. Her skin showed the effects of the cold mountain winters and the heat of the summer sun, and her upper teeth were store-bought, which embarrassed her and brought fond teasing from Big Tate, who still had all his own, top and bottom.

Jed pressed his thumb against the crumbs on the table and licked them off. "So we got to sell the pig to buy us a stove?"

"It's not only the stove, Jed, it's Uncle Caully, too. He's needin' an operation on his leg, and, of course, we'll help out. It goes without sayin'."

So that's the way it would be then. For a

moment, a plate of sausages and hot cakes danced before Jed's eyes, but he refused to dwell on it. He went back into the front room and waited. When he was quite sure his mother was occupied with the bread making, he deftly reached into the small closet and pulled out one of his winter boots. Sticking his hand down inside, he carefully pulled out an object wrapped in newspaper. He passed by his mother unnoticed and went out on the back stoop. Gently, he unwrapped the paper. There was a rough carving of the schoolhouse, made of black walnut. It was far from finished, however. Jed had started it several months before, but there was only the door and the slanted roof. He knew he had several hours of work yet before he could give it to the teacher for a paperweight. He took his knife from his pocket and began working cautiously on the windows.

He was so absorbed in the paperweight that he did not notice the colors of the trees growing dimmer, or the tall, dark mountain turning into the head of a man against the red sky. His father looked in the kitchen window and didn't see him, and he came on around the side of the house, so black with coal grime that his teeth shone out like white buttons.

"I'm waitin,' Jed," he said, throwing his jacket down on the grass.

Jed leaped from the stoop, almost dropping the little schoolhouse. Big Tate came over. "What you workin' on? Looks like girl stuff—a dollhouse or somethin'."

Jed tried to underplay it. "It's a paperweight for the teacher—keep her papers from blowin' when the door opens."

"Mighty fancy paperweight, when a brick'll do as well," Big Tate scoffed.

Jed said nothing, but set his partly finished schoolhouse high on the window ledge.

Big Tate sensed the anger in his silence. "I didn't mean to ride you," he said more gently. "Just think you got good workin' hands—good big hands like mine. Carvin's okay, but it's a small thing, and good hands are meant for big things." He massaged the back of his neck as he spoke and started for the outdoor shower stall.

Jed set his jaw. "Like fightin', I suppose."

Big Tate turned sharply. "Sure—if it comes to that. Boy big as you ought to be able to do better by the Miles boy than waltz him around the grass. . . ."

It was smoldering again—the long battle between Jed and his father—the tersely spoken battle that eeked out between talk of Uncle Caully's operation and when it had rained last and whether there would be rabbit or squirrel for Thanksgiving. And each time the words erupted, the feelings were only half said. Afterward Jed would feel that he and his father were further apart than ever.

It didn't do to explain again that he and Tommy had only been playing around at school. Big Tate wanted to believe something else. He wanted to believe that his grudge against Sedge Miles didn't stop with himself. He wanted to believe that Jed, his only boy, had the makings of a sixth-generation miner. If you asked him if he wanted his son to grow up working the mines as his father and grandfathers had before him, Big Tate would have said no, a mine was the hell hole of the earth, but he wouldn't really mean it. He'd mean yes, of course—where else would a real man prove he was a man?

Jed went into the house without answering. He connected the shower hose to the pump, and without waiting for his father to get in the shower, pumped hard, taking his resentment out on the pump handle. Big Tate glared at him through the window—then thrust his big shoulders under the stream of cold water and lathered up.

Jed watched his father—watched the grime pouring off his hair and showing the white patch again.

Big mountain animal, Jed was thinking,

pushing and pounding his way along in the world, throwing his hulk against the rock face and anything else that got in his way. . . .

He counted forty, but his father was still scrubbing, and he knew he hadn't better stop pumping until his father told him to.

"Enough," came the gruff voice after a bit. Jed grabbed the towel on the chair and went outdoors. He tossed it to his father and started to walk away.

"Jed."

He stopped. "Yeah?"

"What you figurin' to do with yourself, anyway?"

"What do you mean?"

"I mean when you're out of school. You've got to be thinkin'. . . ."

"Don't matter, does it?" Jed retorted. "You don't have to think none to go into the mine—just sort of fall into it. It's there if I want it."

It was smart talk, and Jed was pushing his luck.

"Nobody asked you to get your big white hands dirty!" Big Tate exploded. "All I'm askin' is that you're thinkin' on it."

"I'm not thinkin' on anything. I just wish you'd let me find it out easy."

Big Tate shrugged. "Sure! Sure! Take all

the time in the world. Who's rushing you? But your hands'll never know if they're meant for anything bigger if you never give 'em a try. You can't expect 'em to go from a block of wood one day to a coal seam the next. You're gonna be a man, Jed, you got to try your hands at it."

Now Jed was really angry. "That's the only kind of man there is, huh—a guy what goes under the ground. Anybody else is chicken. Any man does somethin' different ain't worth the name."

"We're five generations, Jed," said his father, spitting out the words. "We're five generations in the mines, and you're the only son I got. If it ain't to be the mines, it's got to be somethin' awful good."

It was no evening to be bitter, however. As soon as Jed saw April Ruth and Bea all dressed up in Sunday blouses, he knew it was the apple peeling.

"The girls invited six young ones over," Mrs. Tate said, tying on a fresh apron. She turned to Jed. "There'll be popcorn too. You can ask two, three of your friends to come."

"Preston Hardy's comin'!" April Ruth said knowingly, glancing at Bea.

"So?" said Beatrice, annoyed. "He comes every year. What's so special about that?"

Big Tate grinned. "He'd be comin' if there was apples or not. Long as Bea's got red in her cheeks, there'll be boys around." He turned to his wife. "How many gallons of apple butter you figure on makin', Lona?"

"Twelve, if they peel a bushel and a half and don't eat most the pieces."

"Jolly's comin', too," April Ruth chattered. "I stopped in the store and told her."

Jed snorted. Jolly had a lot of nerve showing up here after that trick with the pig. He'd get Tommy Miles, and they'd see she got what was coming to her.

Big Tate was trying hard to make up with Jed. He set two big baskets of apples on the back stoop. Picking one of the best from on top, he tossed a big red apple to Jed. "Here's the prettiest of the lot," he said. "Never start an apple peelin' without pickin' the best one and eatin' it through. Gives ya a feeling of how the apple butter's goin' to turn out."

By eight o'clock, the yard was full of friends, and April Ruth helped her mother pop the corn, topped with hot lard and butter. Jolly must have sneaked in the front door, because when Jed turned around, he saw her sticking close to April Ruth.

It was a good time to be on the back stoop that night. Jed and Tommy threw buckeyes at

Jolly's knees when no one was looking, and secretly guffawed at the way Preston Hardy arrived in a starched shirt with big, yellow cuff links.

April Ruth got up for another pitcher of cider, Jolly right behind her.

"Hey, Tommy," Jed said. "How you catch a bear? You have to have a girl for bait, don't you?"

Tommy grinned. "Yeah. But first you got to sweet-talk 'im. First you got to say, 'Here, pretty bear! Here, sweetheart. Here, honey bun.' "

"And then you got to feed it little pieces of fingers—gal's fingers—skinny little gal's fingers to gnaw on. Where we gonna get a skinny little gal, Tommy?" He lunged forward and grabbed at Jolly as she went by, but she squealed and got into the kitchen before he could catch her.

Jed picked up another apple and ran his knife under the skin on top, making a long string of peeling that curled around and around the farther he cut. He tried not to look over at the bench where Bea and Preston Hardy were sitting, but he couldn't help it. It was the silliest thing he ever saw—Preston Hardy sitting there in his striped shirt with the big, yellow cuff links, his pants all pressed and his hair combed slick, picking up apples and handing them to Bea like there was nothing in the world he'd rather do. And every time he dropped one in Bea's lap he sort of leaned over and made his shoulder touch hers. And sometimes she'd drop a piece on the ground, and then they'd both reach down at once to pick it up, and Bea would giggle and their hands would touch and pretty soon they'd do it all over again.

Uncle Caully came up after a bit and sat out on the end of the bench playing his musical saw. "Ahhhh!" he sighed, starting another song. "This one I call, 'Ode to Apple Butter,'" and he ran his bow over the quivering, bent saw between his knees.

"Hey, Uncle Caully," Jed called. "That's an old timer—that's somethin' about a horse. . . ."

"Not if you forget the horse and think apple butter," said Uncle Caully, and everyone laughed.

It wasn't until Uncle Caully stopped playing that Jed realized Bea and Preston were gone, and Bea didn't get home till the yard was empty and the light had gone out in the kitchen.

Saturday morning was even better. Aunt Etta came over early, and Jed hung around the backyard while she and his mother boiled twenty gallons of sweet cider in a huge copper kettle over the outdoor fire. Big Tate and Uncle Caully sat around smoking their pipes and keeping the fire hot, and all day long the young people of Tin Creek trooped by to see if the apple butter was ready for tasting, though they knew it wouldn't be done till evening. When the cider had boiled down to half its amount, Mother and Aunt Etta would add the apples that the young folks had peeled, with sugar and oil of cinnamon, stirring the simmering sauce for hours till it was thick enough to spread. The boys and girls would come back, bringing their own hunks of bread from home, and Mother would put a big glob of apple butter on each slice. Then the women would set about filling the crocks.

The only person to get bored with the apple butter making was April Ruth.

"I'm goin' to the church, Ma, and practice my piano playin'," she called to her mother.

"Ask decent for the key and don't get in the minister's way," her mother called.

April Ruth tucked a copy of "Cherry Pink and Apple Blossom White" under her arm. It was an old piece of sheet music which Aunt Etta had passed on to Lona, and every so often April Ruth would go up to the church and pick it out again on the piano. Then she'd make up her own little tunes which she played mostly on the black keys, since there weren't so many of them and they didn't confuse her the way the white keys did.

Jed waited till she was halfway up the hill to the parsonage. Then he lit out the front door, crossed the dirt road, and scrambled up the hill by the back path to Tommy's house.

Tommy lived in a row of duplex houses, built when the company owned most of the town. The Miles family lived on one side of a duplex painted green, and Mose Hardy and Preston lived in the other half. When Mrs. Hardy was alive, she'd wanted her part of the house pink, and now Mose wasn't about to change it back. It was the only pink and green house in Tin Creek. The part of the yard that belonged to Tommy's father was surrounded by palings—a fence of slender slats which encircled the yard and did its job of keeping people out. But Jed knew which slat would give, and he slipped through.

Sedge Miles was mending a step on his back porch. He startled when Jed came up behind him, and Jed was sorry to find him home.

"What you want, Tate?" he said gruffly. He called all Jed's family "Tate." That was all he needed to know about them, and "Tate" was enough to bring the old grudge boiling to the surface.

54

It was a grudge which had been festering for seventeen years, ever since the day when Jed's grandfather and Tommy's grandfather were working the mine together and the whistle blew. On that day, when the whistle blew in the middle of the morning, it told the people of Tin Creek that there was a fire below, and the wives and children and aunts and grandmothers went running up over the hill to Number 7—up the hill, past the schoolhouse, and to the mine beyond—waiting, like so many relatives before them—for news of the men who were working in the blackness underneath.

Every so often the cage would come clanking up and two or three men who had made their way through the smoke and fire to the shaft would stumble out and into the arms of weeping women. Finally all the men had been accounted for but two—Big Tate's father and Sedge Miles' father, both in their sixties, who had been working farthest down the seam. When the cage came up for the last time, Grandfather Tate was on it—alone. He was sitting slouched down in one corner when they pulled him out, one pants leg burned off and his face and arms the color of coal.

"Where's Potter Miles?" they all asked him. "Where's the other man?"

What Grandfather Tate told them was that

Potter Miles had passed out, and that his own strength was gone. He could barely pull himself to the shaft and get on, and hadn't the energy to drag Potter down the long tunnel with him. When the rescue team went down for Potter, the tunnel had caved in, and Potter Miles was buried forever in the earth below— somewhere under the mountain.

"What you want, Tate?" Sedge Miles said again, frowning at Jed, and Jed knew exactly what he was thinking: Get off my property, Tate, you yellow-legged grandson of a miner that weren't man enough to bring my father up with him. Get off my land, Tate, you grandson of a coward who wasn't strong enough or good enough to carry a better man than he. Get off my ground, boy, and keep away from my son.

"Tommy here?" Jed asked.

Sedge nodded toward the house and went on pounding.

Inside, Tommy's mother was ironing work shirts. A little more friendly, she looked up and said, "Hello, Jed. I hear there's apple-butter makin' at your place today."

Jed nodded. "If it's good, Ma'll send some up." He wasn't sure of that. "Tommy here?"

"Out in front, I reckon."

Jed found Tommy on the front porch, swinging on an old tire that hung from the roof.

"C'mon, Tommy, quick," he said. "Over to the church."

Tommy stared. "Bea gettin' married?"

"No. April Ruth's practicin'. Let's sneak in."

They crossed the Hardys' yard and the Benning sisters', and cut through the houses on bosses' row, sliding down the hill into the little hollow behind, where the small, white church nestled among the pines, and farther on, the parsonage.

As they tiptoed up the three white steps, they could hear the plink plunk of piano keys. Carefully they wedged open the door and slipped inside. They crawled along till they reached the back pew and wriggled underneath it, lying flat on their stomachs, smirking as April Ruth laboriously picked out the notes of "Cherry Pink and Apple Blossom White."

Before Jed could decide what to do, now that they were here, the playing stopped and the piano bench creaked. He cautiously peered around the edge of the pew. April Ruth was standing up.

"Ladies and gentlemen," she said.

Jed and Tommy stared at each other. But April Ruth went no further. She came down the aisle to the back of the church, peered out the door, then closed it again. She walked back up to the piano at the front, and Jed and Tommy lay like dead men.

"Ladies and gentlemen," April Ruth said again. "I have the great privilege of introducing the finest young piano player in West Virginia—a girl who didn't have no piano lessons till she was almost growed, but who used to practice on a piano in a little church back in Tin Creek, makin' up her own songs . . . ."

Jed's mouth fell open.

". . . and now she stands before you all," April Ruth continued, "the greatest piano player of all, playin' her own compositions— April Ruth Tate!"

Jed rolled around under the pew, struggling to keep from laughing. He stuffed one fist in his mouth, and every time he looked at Tommy, who was doing the same, their bodies shook with silent laughter.

The piano began again, a tune, Jed thought, that sounded a little like "Flow Gently Sweet Afton," but not quite. Whatever it was, April Ruth played it better than she had "Cherry Pink and Apple Blossom White." Then she did her own version of "Hark the Herald Angels Sing." Jed decided she wasn't too bad.

"And now," said April Ruth, standing up again, "for an encore, Miss Tate will play. . . ."

58

They never found out, for at the words, "Miss Tate," Jed let loose an uncontrollable guffaw that shattered the four walls of the church and stopped the chatter instantly.

For a moment, the church was so still that Jed felt he could hear the mice in the basement. Then he saw Tommy rolling around under the pew, his hands over his mouth, and Jed exploded with another great gust of laughter, Tommy joining in with high squeals.

"Jed Jefferson Tate!" April Ruth screamed.

In an instant she was down the aisle after them. The boys scrambled out from beneath the seats and went leaping over the pews. Around and around they went, the boys yelling with laughter, April Ruth's cheeks crimson, tears rising furiously in her eyes. After a few minutes, Jed and Tommy took refuge behind the pulpit to catch their breath, instantly ready to spring and separate the minute April Ruth reached them.

But suddenly the lights went out. They heard the rattle of the latch, and then the front door slammed. There were footsteps outside and then silence.

It didn't seem fair for her to give up so easily. Jed stood up and grinned sheepishly at Tommy.

"Short concert, huh!" Tommy said, and

they laughed again. They went over to the piano and played chopsticks together and then made "thunder" on the low keys and "lightning" on the high keys.

"The *great* April Ruth Tate!" said Jed, and they laughed.

It was time to check on the apple butter again, so they closed the lid over the keys and went back to the door. Jed tried the handle. It wouldn't move. He put both hands on the knob and pushed. The door was locked from the outside.

"*She* did it!" said Tommy.

"She took the key back to the parsonage, and I'll bet she didn't even tell 'em we was in here!" said Jed.

"Huh! We'll git out a window." Tommy went over to a window and raised the blue glass panel. Every window had a piece of wire screen nailed to the frame outside. There was no way out except to push through the screen, and they knew better than to do that. They were here until April Ruth decided to come and get them, and it probably wouldn't be until bedtime, at least.

"And then she'll only do it to keep Ma from worryin'," said Jed, beginning to get mad. "Stupid old thing—can't even take a joke. All we was doin' was listening."

"You think if we holler anybody'll come?"
Tommy wondered.

"Who's gonna hear? Parsonage is a quarter mile away. Besides, April might be out in
the trees somewhere just waitin' to hear us
scream and preparin' to enjoy it. I won't let
her know it's botherin'."

Church on Sunday was one thing, but
church on Saturday afternoon with apple butter cooking in the backyard was another. The
more the boys thought about it, the more they
wanted out. Mrs. Miles would figure Tommy
was at the Tates' all afternoon, and there would
be so many folks at the Tates' that Jed's ma
wouldn't know if he was around or not.

"April's really mad now," Jed said ruefully, knowing what it would be like when they
got out. "You watch. She'll kill us."

They stood at the side window, unable to
see the road, and listened for sounds that might
mean somebody walking by. But it was a long
way up to bosses' row on one side, and nothing
but fields on the other. Old Mr. Morgan, the
circuit minister, always slept on Saturday afternoons, and there was no reason for anybody
else to be down this way.

Jed's stomach told him again that he was
hungry, and now he began to get mad. He could
just see April Ruth returning that key to the

minister's wife, smiling real sweet and saying thanks for letting her use the piano. And all the while, Mrs. Morgan thought she was such a blessed child. Oh, how he hated her, hated her, *hated* her. She was probably sitting in the backyard right now slopping a big spoonful of warm apple butter on some of Ma's fresh-made bread, grinning and licking her fingers.

The shadows lengthened, and the sun dipped behind the hill. Now Ma and Aunt Etta would be thinking about supper, and they'd bring out some cold roast chicken and fry up some potatoes and throw some apples in a pan with bread crumbs and brown sugar, and serve it warm with cream. And April Ruth would just sit there with cream dribbling down her chin smiling to herself and acting real surprised when everybody said where's Jed?

There was the sound of light footsteps on the ground outside. Jed jumped up, ready to yell, when he heard a key fumble in the lock. So she'd come back! So she'd come to make them say they were sorry before she'd let them out! He'd jump her. He'd knock the key right out of her hand.

The front door opened and in came Jolly Parsons.

"Mighty Moses!" said Tommy. "Look what came to rescue us, Jed."

"How'd you know we was here, Jolly?" Jed asked, truly glad to see her.

"Promise you won't tell?"

"Promise."

"April Ruth told me when she went by the store. She was so mad she was spittin' nails out both sides her mouth. She said she wasn't lettin' you out till just before service tomorrow morning. So I went to the parsonage and told Mrs. Morgan I left my Sunday sweater on the bench, and she let me have the key. Make like you climbed out a window or something, or April Ruth'll never speak to me again."

Like rabbits out of a pen, Jed and Tommy sprinted out the door.

"She'll never know it from us," Jed promised.

With hands in their pockets, they sauntered jauntily home, thinking up a good one to tell April Ruth. Jolly was okay—her and her toothpick legs—in spite of the pig.

Chapter Four

April Ruth wasn't home when Jed got there. He was disappointed. He'd wanted to see her face when he walked in.

The apple butter was done, and Mother was dipping it into crocks. Tommy stayed long enough to eat three slices of bread smeared heavily with the reddish butter. Then, when it was obvious that April Ruth had gone to a friend's house, he went on home. Mrs. Tate did not offer to send any butter home with him.

The big disappointment was that supper

64

was cold. It consisted of government commodities bought at Parsons' with food stamps —cold tinned beef and boiled rice. The stove was broken and there were no fried potatoes and no Brown Betty either. Jed ate silently while the grown-ups talked it out.

"I can drive over to Fairmont and pick you up a stove Monday," Uncle Caully said, hoisting his bad leg up on a chair. "How high you want to go, Sam?"

Big Tate folded a slice of bread over a cold slab of beef. "How much we got in the box, Lona?"

"Eighty-one," said Mother, without even looking. "All that's goin' for the operation, and then some. And Christmas is comin'. That's why we got to sell the pig."

Big Tate sighed—a sort of low, hidden sigh that seemed to travel right down his chest and back up through his lips again.

"I hate to see the pig go just 'cause my leg is needin' care," Caully said. "I could put it off past New Year's."

"You're talkin' out of your head," Big Tate said to his brother. "You got to have the operation and we got to have us a stove, so the pig's got to be sold. Take it to Fairmont with you, Caully, and see what you can get. Don't go higher'n sixty on the stove, you can help it."

"It's got to have four burners and a two-shelf oven," said Mother.

"I'll take my time and get the best deal I can," Caully promised.

There went the breakfast sausages and the pork roast and hams and scrapple.

Big Tate silently munched his bread sandwich. He watched Jed across the table and knew what he was thinking. "Aw, heck, Jed, that old pig was more trouble'n it was worth." He grinned. "Why, pretty soon Caully'd have to come and git the whole danged school after the varmint, and the neighbors'd git so mad at it trampin' down the flowers, they'd come and like as not slaughter it at night while we was asleep."

Jed smiled back but said nothing. If his own secret plan worked, they'd have pork roast three times a year instead of one. And sausages every Sunday, if they wanted it. All he had to do was get to Morgantown before December 15. It all had to do with the hidden things in the boot in the closet.

It was almost nine-thirty before April Ruth came home. Mother and Father and Uncle Caully and Aunt Etta were in the front room— the men playing checkers over by the radio.

Jed heard her steps on the porch. He stretched out lazily on the cot behind the coal stove and slowly bit into an apple, rubbing his toes together.

The screen door opened and April Ruth came in, dropping her sweater on the old green couch.

"We have supper yet?" she asked.

"There's beef and cold rice Etta brought," said her mother.

April Ruth paused. "Uh . . . Jed home?"

Mrs. Tate nodded toward the cot and went on talking.

April Ruth wheeled around and stared behind the stove. Jed couldn't control the grin which spread across his face, and he bit into the apple again, licking at the juice that oozed down his chin.

April Ruth's cheeks turned scarlet, and her eyes looked like two coals in the bottom of the stove. Without speaking, she walked on past him and into the kitchen. When Jed started out for the pump a moment later, April Ruth had her head down on her arms, and she was crying!

Silently Jed backed up and went to the cot again. She wasn't as mad as she was embarrassed—ashamed that Jed and Tommy had seen her acting out her dream. Well, what was so wrong about a dream? He had one, too, didn't he?

On Monday, Jed took the paperweight to school. He had worked on it all Sunday afternoon and evening, carving it just right and tucking in under the steps whenever anybody walked by. Now it was done—not quite as he'd hoped it would turn out, but pretty good.

He hung back at recess and waited till Tommy and Jolly had gone out to start a game of Red Rover. Then, when Miss Singer was erasing the sentences on the blackboard, he went up to her desk and put the black walnut schoolhouse on the pile of arithmetic papers.

It looked so real that he almost saw the door opening. It looked like a real log school sitting on a white snowy field, and it was big enough and strong enough to hold down the whole pile of papers without tipping over. He was halfway to the door when she called him.

"Jed?"

He stopped and turned around. Miss Singer was standing by the desk in her soft blue dress, holding the paperweight in her hands.

"Jed? Did you put this here?"

He swallowed. "Yes, ma'am?"

"Is it for me? Where did you get it?"

He fidgeted uncomfortably. "It's a paper-weight—to keep the pages from blowin' all around. I made it."

Miss Singer looked at the schoolhouse and turned it around and around in her hands. "You *made* it, Jed? You carved it out?"

"Yes, ma'am."

"Why, Jed, it's good! Really good!" Miss Singer sat down and put the paperweight on the desk in front of her, looking at it carefully. "I never knew you could carve so well. Do you make a lot of things?"

Jed beamed with pleasure. Should he tell her about the others? "Oh, I carve some now and then." No, he wouldn't. She might say they were good, but not good enough to win first prize in Morgantown.

Miss Singer smiled at him—a warm smile, as if she really liked him, and liked the paper-weight. "I'm awfully pleased with it. It was thoughtful of you to make it for me. It's hard to believe you had no help. Sure your dad didn't do some of it for you?"

"No, ma'am. I did it all."

He went out on the playground with his chest bursting. He felt great.

Monday evening was like Christmas already. Uncle Caully came back from Fairmont in his pickup with a secondhand stove like none other. It was bright yellow, the color of buttercups, and it had a little handle on top that was set to ticking for as long as there was a pie in the oven, and a bell would ring when the pie was done.

"You'll never believe it!" said Caully, chuckling like Santa himself. "I sold the pig, bought the stove, and had enough left over to buy two smoked hams. There'll be pork for Thanksgiving and Christmas too, and I even got some sausage for hot cakes Sunday." Jed suspected that Uncle Caully had bought the sausage with his own money, and probably the hams as well, but the family was in a festive mood.

Aunt Etta came up to look at the stove and brought some pie dough with her. She and his mother got to giggling like schoolgirls over the yellow stove with the ticker on top. Pretty soon they'd rolled out a dozen apple dumplings to try it out, and everyone sat around listening for the timer. When the bell rang, they looked in the oven, and the dumplings were golden brown and sizzling, just the way they should be.

Lona Tate was happy. The pink showed up in her cheeks, and she even sat down on Father's lap for a minute, while he circled her with his two great brown arms—something they didn't do very often.

Big Tate was feeling soft toward his son, too. "Have another dumplin', Jed," he said, sliding the warm pan across the table. "Best while they're hot."

Jed needed no second invitation. There was cream to go on the dumplings, and Jed felt glad in his home that night.

October slipped by, and Big Tate began bathing inside when he came up from the mine. He would strip down to his waist and—with long johns flopping down his back—he'd kneel down and dip his head and arms and shoulders in the big galvanized tub on the kitchen floor. When he was clean down to his waist, Mother would close the kitchen door, and he'd climb in the tub and sit down.

Early in November, Uncle Caully went to the hospital in Charleston. Big Tate drove him there on a Sunday and stayed Monday for the operation, taking time off work. Aunt Etta went with him. She would live with her sister until Caully was well enough to come back home.

It had been almost a year since Uncle Caully had injured his leg in a mine accident, and now he drew the worker's compensation which kept him and Etta going—that, plus her pay as postmistress of Tin Creek and the little bit Caully earned from painting and repair work. Last summer the doctor had looked at Caully's leg again, and this time he'd said Caully needed an operation. But he couldn't prove that what was wrong with Caully's leg this time had anything to do with the injury in the mine, so the mining company didn't have to pay for the operation. It was up to Caully himself and his brother Sam.

All Monday evening Jed and his mother and sisters listened for the sound of Uncle Caully's pickup truck. When they finally heard it at ten o'clock, grinding up the dirt road, they went to the door and waited for Big Tate.

He came in the room and took off his jacket. Jed had never seen his father's mouth sag as it did; the deep lines reaching down into his chin. He stood by the door, rubbing the back of his neck to ease the tension.

"He lost the leg, Lona," he said finally. "Fair near up to the hip, it went."

"Sam!" Mother stood without moving. Finally she asked softly, "How is Etta taking it?"

"Real good. Real good. Maybe she figured he was due to lose it. She's a right strong woman." He followed her out to the kitchen where his supper was waiting. But he couldn't seem to eat. He sat with his head in his powerful hands, elbows resting on the table. "The Tates have given three men to the mines, and now Caully's leg as well. It's like a beast, it is—eatin' its fill of every man it can get. A hell hole, that's what—not a fit place for a human creature."

Jed listened silently. It was what his father always said when a man got hurt. Tomorrow he'd go back to the mine as always, and if the tunnels caved in and caught all the men but Father, he'd be wanting to go back the next day.

"I've made up my mind, then," Lona said. "I'm goin' up to bosses' row and ask the ladies can I do their wash. We got to have us some more money, and one of the foremen's wives said she could use some help."

"You got all the wash you can handle now, Ma," Big Tate said tenderly.

"Another couple loads won't break my back," said Lona.

Jed went to bed with his throat tight. He tried to imagine Uncle Caully with a wooden leg or one of those stiff mechanical things he saw once in Fairmont. Somehow it didn't fit Uncle Caully, and he went to sleep with his stomach hurting.

There wasn't much Thanksgiving at the Tates' because Uncle Caully wasn't due home till December 20. But Jed wasn't waiting for Thanksgiving—he was waiting for something else. And on the first day of December, Mother said it: "We're going to Morgantown for the sales, Jed—Bea and April Ruth and me. You figure you want to come?"

How do you say yes without leaping up in the air and making a half-turn?

"You'll have to stick by us close, now, and not get lost," Mrs. Tate said. "We're goin' Saturday and takin' the bus."

Patiently Jed waited the week out. He got his old notebook from behind the rose-colored curtain in the front closet and seached for the dog-eared announcement he'd kept pressed between the pages for so many months:

13th Annual Art Sculpture Contest
Sponsored by the Horace Bookstore and the
Morgantown Arts Society
Original entries of plaster, wood, bronze, clay,
etc. must be received no later than
December 15.
First prize $100
Second prize $50
Third prize $25
Winners will be notified by mail
after January 4.

He stretched out on his cot, the notice beneath his pillow, and thought about it all over again. Three prizes, and he had three entries. Surely he would win one. He still remembered the sculpture he'd seen in a Morgantown store last summer when he went with Aunt Etta. There were skinny wire people with hardly any heads at all, crazy looking horses carved of wood, with only three legs maybe, and necks so long they looked like giraffes. There weren't but one or two things that looked the way they ought to, Jed had decided, and not a one that looked as real as the carvings Jed had done.

On Friday night, Bea washed her hair and did it all up funny with little pieces of paper which she twisted around her finger and stuck around each curl.

"For heaven's sake, what you starin' at, Jed?" Bea asked, annoyed.

"At the way them papers are stickin' out all over your head," Jed answered, watching from the cot. "You don't think the wind'll blow 'em all out when you get to Morgantown?"

Bea thumped down her brush disgustedly. "I never! Such a idiot! The papers come out when it's dry, stupid. You think I'm going to Morgantown like this?"

Jed didn't know. Wasn't any worse than the time she did around her eyes with his black watercolors, and the paint ran down her

75

cheeks. Bea was looking more like a grown woman every day, and she kept to herself, fussing with her eyes or her fingernails, or slipping out of the house when Preston Hardy came over.

Preston Hardy had bought an old car from a man in Grafton the week before, and if he didn't think it was something, the way he came rattling down the road and sort of shuddered to a stop outside the house, pumping the gas pedal up and down and frowning at the dashboard and pulling the knobs in and out. One of the doors wouldn't shut right, and the trunk wouldn't lock, but Preston thought it was great. And then Bea would go out and act real interested, and sometimes Preston would even show her under the hood—as if she cared! Finally they'd go chugging off down the road and a couple hours later Bea would come back all uppity, like she'd been to a real restaurant or something, when like as not all they'd done was drive around the high school or up the road through the cemetery.

"You don't stop starin', I won't buy your Christmas present tomorrow," Bea said, gathering up her comb and pins. "What you want for Christmas, anyway?"

"A knife. Not a penknife, but a jackknife."

Bea stood up and examined her face closely

in the little hand mirror, scowling at the way her nose turned up at the end as though she'd just discovered it. "You're always carvin', but I never see nothing you done. What do you do, anyway? Carve it down to chips and throw it away?"

"Oh, I got a couple of things I'm workin' on," Jed said, turning over on his cot. "Maybe I'll show you sometime when they're done."

It was no use waiting for Bea to go to bed now. She was staying up till her hair got dry, and she'd be sitting out here near the stove to keep warm.

Jed pulled the blanket up around him and thought about the prize money. What if he won first prize? Why, he'd give twenty-five dollars to Ma and twenty-five to Pa and still have fifty left over for himself. His mind boggled with the thought of what he could do with a hundred dollars. Or what if he won second prize or even third? And then, as it always did, his dream ended with the unheard of possibility that maybe, just maybe, he'd win all three prizes! One hundred and seventy-five dollars! Enough to buy a new pig and a carload of dresses for Ma and the girls. It was too much to think about. Even he knew it couldn't happen. He watched Bea with heavy eyes, sitting in the rocker by the stove, pushing herself with one foot, and reading the old movie magazine she'd bought in Morgantown last year. Let him win a prize—any prize—and he'd buy her the ten best movie magazines he could find!

He awoke Saturday morning before dawn —even before Big Tate stirred in the small bedroom in the back. His eyes were open instantly, and he threw off his blanket, groping toward the closet and reaching far down inside his winter boots near the back. Carefully he pulled out an old undershirt from one and a wad of newspaper from the other and unwrapped them on his cot. The undershirt contained a little wooden man sitting on a log with a fiddle across his knees and also a meticulous carving of Uncle Caully's old hay wagon with one wheel missing, tilting down at the corner. And in the old newspaper was the pig, carved out of white pine—fat and egg-shaped—the one Jed liked best of all. Somehow, as he stared at them there on his blanket, they didn't look quite as great as he'd remembered them, but still good enough to get a prize. He stuffed the hay wagon in one pocket of his jacket and the wooden man in the other. There wasn't room for the pig, too, so he put that in the hip pocket of his pants. Then he went out to the kitchen to wash, wanting to be the first one ready for Morgantown.

They caught the bus on the new road at nine-fifteen, after Big Tate had left for the mine. There was overtime work on Saturday sometimes, and he worked whenever he could.

After all the work Bea had done on her hair the night before, she had a scarf around her head and her coat collar turned up around her ears. But April Ruth stood there in the wind, her legs red from the cold, grinning like a jack rabbit and humming "April Showers." Mother had promised her she could buy some sheet music if she found any for less than fifty cents, and it was all April Ruth wanted. Jed stood straight, like a soldier on sentry duty, with his pockets bulging, afraid to bend for fear he'd break the delicately carved handle on the hay wagon.

Bea noticed when they got on the bus.

"For heaven's sake, Ma," she whispered as they took the seat behind Jed and April Ruth. "What's he got in his pockets? His lunch?"

"What you got in your pockets, Jed?" Mrs. Tate asked, dropping her change back in her purse and rapping April Ruth on the shoulder for drawing pictures in the steam on the windows.

"Just stuff," said Jed, sitting stiffly. "It's nothin' to you, Bea."

"Just once I wish we could go somewhere without lookin' like a bunch of gypsies," Bea complained. "Mother, look at April! Make her quit."

Mrs. Tate rapped April Ruth on the shoulder again. "Give me that gum, girl. Who gave you bubble gum, land sakes! The Parsons' girl?"

Everything was gray outside the window —the road, the ground, the trees, the sky. They passed the old house with the door on the side and the porch removed—a crazy door that just stepped off into nowhere, and another house near the road where a very old woman always sat smiling at nothing. There were secondhand stores with racks of clothing on the porches, and the old remains of houses without any people in them at all. They rode under the black wood timbers of the railroad bridge, where the cars full of coal passed through the countryside, taking the coal and the money from it to the people on the outside. A big coal truck rumbled by the bus and then another, and the bus driver and the truck drivers made a sort of salute to each other. Then they were passing the signs that said "Say Yes to God" and "Jesus Saves and Keeps," and finally they were out on an open stretch of road and going sixty. Now and then the road led through the business district of a small village, and a Christmas wreath on a lamp post or a big red Santa on a gas station would spot the gray landscape with a touch of color. Jed didn't care how gray it looked—he felt all red and orange and yellow inside.

April Ruth was humming "April Showers" again and picking out the tune on her knees as though they were a keyboard.

"How much do you suppose it costs to go to the university at Morgantown, Jed?" she asked suddenly.

Jed shrugged. " 'Bout a million dollars."

"Not a *million*. Hardly anybody'd be able to go." She turned around. "Ma, how much do you suppose it would cost to go to the university at Morgantown long enough to get a music teachin' certificate or somethin'?"

"A lot more'n we got," Mrs. Tate replied.

"What you mean—a certificate?" Bea said. "You've got to get yourself a degree—that's four years."

"Four years! Four years of college learnin' to play the piano?" April Ruth exclaimed.

"If you want to teach it—like at a school or somethin'."

April Ruth leaned back against the seat, her eyes squinting out over the fields.

" 'Course, if you just want to learn good enough to give lessons to the folks in Tin Creek, suppose you could just learn from somebody yourself and not go to college at all," Bea told her.

Jed sat very still. He could almost hear

April Ruth's dream bursting—the one she'd been carrying around in secret until Jed and Tommy discovered it. The greatest piano player in the state of West Virginia wouldn't spend the rest of her life giving music lessons to the children in Tin Creek. April Ruth didn't move either. She wiped her arm across her eyes and turned her face toward the window.

Christmas decorations were up in Morgantown. People hurried by outside the bus with shopping bags and wrapping paper, and students from the university bantered with each other as they crowded the sidewalks in groups. As the bus pulled into the depot, Mrs. Tate leaned forward and grabbed Jed's arm.

"Listen good, Jed. We got to catch the 3:10 bus to get home in time for Pa's supper. Don't you go wanderin' off at the last minute. You stick by."

Jed nodded.

Mrs. Tate took off down the sidewalk with Bea a few steps behind her and April Ruth and Jed following in a line, like a mother duck and her young. Mrs. Tate headed right for the department store that was having the sale, and it was there, in the bargain basement, that she always bought all the Christmas presents for the family and relatives. Sometimes she'd lead the children around to one counter or another,

82

getting their opinions on things they'd like, and then she'd send them over to a far corner of the store while she made her purchases. Christmas presents were never a complete surprise that way, but at least there was no money wasted.

All the way to the store, Jed watched the names of the cross streets, looking for Willey Street and the Horace Bookshop. But he didn't see it, and began to worry. Somehow he'd thought he'd find it right away. Somehow he'd thought he'd slip off when Mother had her back turned and enter his carvings in the contest. Now Morgantown stretched out before him, blocks and blocks of stores and shops, with side streets angling off at every intersection.

At the department store, Mrs. Tate and her daughters went to the ladies' section and looked at sweaters. "Look around, Jed, and see if you can find a present for Pa," said his mother. "He could use a new checkerboard— maybe some work socks."

Jed couldn't find any checkerboards so he went to men's wear and bought some socks, size 13. He was going to buy a pair for Uncle Caully too, till he remembered his leg. As the clerk gave him his change, Jed asked about Willey Street, and the Horace Bookstore.

"It's about ten blocks up, near the university," the clerk said. "Better take a bus."

Jed gulped. "I got to walk."

"Look here then." The clerk took a paper bag and drew a map on it. "Here's where you are—at the X. You've got to go up to the corner, turn left, go six blocks, turn right, and go three."

Jed put the directions in his jacket pocket. How could he possibly get way up there and back again without Mother knowing? He wandered around the basement. He bought a bracelet for Bea and some lipstick and powder sets on sale for his mother and Aunt Etta. He couldn't see anything at all for April Ruth.

It was midafternoon before they thought of eating, and as always they went to the Hav-a-Lunch on Pleasant Street, where the cooking was about as good as Aunt Etta's, and you could get soup and big hunks of homemade bread for thirty cents.

Jed sat on the stool at the lunch counter, mauling his bread and trying to figure out how to get away.

"I wouldn't have to go back to the store," he said finally. "I'm all finished with my shoppin'. I could look around the street."

"And wander off," said his mother.

"No I won't. You tell me where you want me to be, and I'll be there any time you say."

84

"You haven't got a watch."

"There's clocks around. I'll ask every few minutes. . . ."

"Jed Jefferson Tate, if you miss that bus. . . ."

"Just tell me where and what time," Jed pleaded.

Mother thought it over. "All right. I want you to be right here in forty-five minutes. Three o'clock. You understand?"

"Three o'clock, right here," Jed said.

"And don't wander off so far you can't get yourself back."

"I won't." Jed stuffed his bread in his mouth and gulped down the rest of his soup. He picked up his packages and walked leisurely out the door. As soon as he was out of sight, he pulled the directions to Willey Street out of his pocket and began running as fast as he could.

It was nine blocks away. A city block had never seemed so long to Jed before, and it was all up hill. By the time he had run five, he had a pain in his side and had to walk.

There was a clock in a beauty parlor as he passed that read two-twenty. He started to run again, his chest heaving.

It was two-thirty when he reached Willey Street. He dug in his pocket for the contest announcement to get the number of the bookstore and ran three more blocks before he found it.

He opened a door and a bell jangled. At first it seemed there was no one there. Jed waited nervously. There were shelves at the back of the store with the sculpture of local artists on them—the strange funny wire people and the faceless animals and the blobs and squares and circles that didn't seem to mean anything at all.

There was a shuffling in the back room and a man came out, apparently finishing his lunch. "Yes?" he said, coughing and wiping his mouth at the same time.

"I came about the contest," Jed said. He set his packages on the counter, and began pulling the wooden carvings from his three pockets.

The man stared at them. "What was it you wanted?"

"The contest," Jed said. "I want to enter these."

"Oh." The man stared a minute longer and then went to his desk and took out a paper. "Your name?"

"Jed Jefferson Tate."

"T-A-T-E?"

"Yes."

"How old are you, Jed?"

"Goin' on twelve."

"Live around here?"

"Tin Creek." Jed gave the address.

"What do you call them?"

"What?"

"The sculpture. Does it have a title? Do you want them entered separately or as a group?"

Jed's head swam. "I don't know," he said. "They don't have no names or nothin'."

"Well, that's all right. Let's enter them as a group, and we'll call it *Americana*. Okay?"

Jed waited a moment, hating to leave them so abruptly. His eye caught a big table on one side of the store with a sign which read, "Assorted sheet music. Collectors' items. Four for $1.00." Just what April Ruth wanted!

Jed hurried over and instantly his eyes found a copy of "April Showers." He could hardly believe it. This was his lucky day. He glanced up at the clock. It was a quarter of three. His heart began to race. He rummaged quickly through the music on the table. He couldn't decide between "Goodnight, Irene" and "White Christmas." He finally decided on "White Christmas" and paid the man fifty cents for the two. Then he hurried from the store in a near run. He couldn't stop for an instant if he expected to be on time.

He was almost three blocks from the bookstore when he realized he'd left his other packages back on the counter. Giving a little cry, he whirled around and dashed across the street again to the blowing of horns. He raced frantically back up the sidewalk to the bookstore, bolted inside, grabbed his packages from the counter, and dashed out again. The clock on the wall said five minutes to three.

Jed couldn't even think as he ran back again. There was no excuse possible. He'd made a promise and broken it. The pain in his side stabbed at him as he ran, but he couldn't stop. On he went, weaving in and out of traffic, dodging the crowds on the sidewalk. By the time he passed the clock in the beauty parlor again it read five after three, and by the time he got to the Hav-a-Lunch, the big hand was on two.

She was sitting at the counter alone, her arms full of packages, her shoulders hunched, like a greyhound ready to spring. There was no sign of Bea or April Ruth.

Their eyes met instantly. A mixture of fury and relief crossed his mother's face, and she sprang to her feet, bolting out the door toward the bus stop, with Jed behind her.

"Ma, I'm sorry, I'm sorry!" Jed began miserably. But there was no time to explain. There was still the possibility that the bus was there, and together they ran, packages and all, down Pleasant Street and around the corner to the bus station.

The bus had just gone. Mrs. Tate had sent the girls on home to get supper for their father. The next bus was at five thirty-five.

They sat down on a bench near the back of the waiting room, side by side. Never had Jed felt worse. His mother was so angry she dared not speak, and Jed could tell by the way her fingers pressed against each other just how deep the anger went.

"Ma, I'm really sorry," Jed began again.

She didn't answer.

"I mean it."

She started to speak, but stopped. Then she started again. "You said you'd be back. You promised!"

"I tried! I did! Somethin' happened . . ."

She looked at him furiously. "*What* happened?"

"I left my packages somewhere. I had to go back."

"Good lord, wouldn't you know it! Where? How far away did you go?"

Jed took a deep breath. He had to tell her. He owed her that much.

"A bookstore . . . over by the university. I wanted it to be . . . a surprise, like."

The anger was giving away. She was resigned now to sitting in the bus station another two hours. "Tell me, Jed," she said.

Jed's voice was shaky. "It was a contest I heard about," he began. "Last summer when Aunt Etta and me was in Morgantown, I found some notices about it in the drugstore—a sculpture contest goin' on at the Horace Bookstore, first prize one hundred dollars, with second and third prizes too, and I entered three things I done. . . ."

Lona Tate stared at her son. "You entered a contest? Somethin' you been workin' on? The paperweight that looked like a schoolhouse?"

"Ma, these were a lot better'n that paperweight." Jed's eyes sparkled. "I done them real good. I been savin' 'em in the closet in my boots and didn't nobody know. Ma, if I git that one hundred dollars, we're goin' to have another Christmas in January. They'll be writin' me tellin' did I win, the man said."

Lona Tate shook her head, the faintest smile on her lips.

"Jed, it was Christmas just to see you walk in that lunchroom, mad as I was. You don't know all the things I thought had happened to you. You and your big ideas. I swear it. Why didn't you show 'em to me?"

"I didn't want anybody talkin' me out of it. Besides, you'd show 'em to Pa."

90

"It would've been so bad?"

"You know what he'd say."

Mrs. Tate was silent a moment. "Maybe," she said finally.

They sat together in the back row. Lona gave him a dime to put in the machine, and they shared a package of cheese crackers.

"You and April Ruth and your dreams of glory," Mrs. Tate said at last, slipping off her shoes and leaning heavily on the packages beside her. "You both got hands that want to be doin', and it's the kind of things Tin Creek don't know much about."

Chapter Five

Jed's mother didn't let on about the contest.

"Just like him to leave his packages some place," Bea commented. "I told you he shouldn't have gone off alone, Ma. Kid hasn't sense enough to come in out of the rain."

"Forgetful, maybe, but he's got sense," Mrs. Tate said, and Bea kept quiet.

Big Tate was in no mood to hear about the trip to Morgantown. The girls had given him his supper, and now he sat slumped down in his chair by the radio, scowling at nobody in particular, while Mrs. Tate and Jed ate their supper cold. Later, when Lona got out the ironing board and started in on the boss's laundry, Pa said, "It's a good thing you've bought the presents already, 'cause there might not be a Christmas otherwise."

"What do you mean, Sam?" Mrs. Tate paused with the iron in her hand.

"Sedge Miles is stirrin' up talk about strikin' again, an' might call a meetin' of the union. Says the company ain't keepin' its promise to rock-dust. Hell, that ain't news. But leave it to Sedge to bring it up right before Christmas."

Jed lay still on the cot.

He knew what that meant, all right. Rock-dusting kept down the coal dust in the mines. If there was too much dust, there were explosions in the tunnels.

Mrs. Tate brought the iron down again on the shirt collar before her. "I'd rather have you here for Christmas than all the dresses in Morgantown," she said simply. "If there's dust in the mine and the company won't rock-dust, then you ought to strike. Sedge is right."

It galled Big Tate to hear her say that. It angered him to think that after all these years of living with the hate he held for Sedge Miles, Lona could say a good word about him.

"You don't see the point of it," he said, his

voice sharp, his shoulders hunched like a big, gray animal. "Number 7's 'bout mined out, Lona! One more year and it's through! Then we've got to find us another mine, or go on welfare. We strike now and they'll close up Number 7 and go on workin' 8 and 10. No sweat to them. We ain't that important."

"You are to me," said Lona flatly, and Jed listened. "It's more'n once I've thought of you trapped down there under the mountain, not ever to come out, and if it happened, Sam—I swear it—Christmas wouldn't never be Christmas again for me."

Her words soothed him a little, and he leaned back, watching her work. "You've worries enough without takin' on that too, Lona," he said gently. "It's only half the time I'm under the mountain. Last week we were workin' the seam right under Tin Creek. Why, if I'd had a ladder, I could've come right up through the kitchen."

Jed's mother smiled a little. "You take it light, Sam—and that's a man's way, I guess. But it's a worry I got to keep."

Uncle Caully came home on the sixteenth. Big Tate drove the pickup truck to Charleston on Sunday and brought him and Etta back.

"Caully's home now," Sam said, sticking

his head in the door of his own house. "Let's go over and see him."

Jed dreaded it. As he walked down the road beside his father, he wondered what he would say to Uncle Caully.

"You suppose he's sour about it, Pa?" Jed asked suddenly.

Big Tate walked on, taking big strides. "Don't seem to be. Reckon he can't help but be some."

"Would you be, if it was you?" Jed ventured.

"I might, for a time, maybe, but I'd get over it. You go in the mine and that's the chance you take. You can't go through life thinkin' what might have been. That kind of thinkin' just makes you sick."

That was true, and Jed knew his father meant it. But wasn't it okay to think what things might *be*—what the mines might be if all the safety regulations were really enforced, what Tin Creek would look like without the slag pile and the sludge oozing down into the hollow and the silt filling up the creek bed and making it flood in the spring?

He needn't have worried about what to say to Caully. His uncle was in a chair with a blanket over his lap, and his big face was all smiles. He was glad to be back.

95

"Jed, what you been eatin' since I been away, uh? You lost a pound in each cheek!" He reached out and hugged Jed with his big arms. "You should'a been with me, boy. I would've kept you under the bed and given you half my tray. Why, it was like a hotel! Every day, see, the nurse comes in all starched and pretty and gives me a menu, mind you! Here I am flat on my back, and I'm pickin' out dinner for the next day! 'So you've been a miner, Mr. Tate!' she says to me. 'Well, I want to see you eat like one.' So every day, besides the meat and potatoes I'm writin' down on the menu, she brings me soup and pie and ice cream and milk, besides the coffee. Why, I'm like to burst!"

"Caully, it's good to have you back," Mrs. Tate said. "Christmas wouldn't be anything without you."

"It's sure good to be home," Caully said, stretching out his one good leg under the blanket. "Why, it's like tryin' to take a nap in a boiler factory, tryin' to sleep in a hospital, I tell you. All night long the attendants are bangin' and jokin' and hustlin' pans up and down the halls, and long 'bout mornin', when you're just ready to fall asleep, they're in your room the crack of dawn to take your tempera-

96

ture and change the sheets, and purty soon they're at you with breakfast again."

They laughed.

"Uncle Caully, your presents are all wrapped and under the tree," April Ruth said, hugging him. "Dad says you got to get your crutches and come up for Christmas—it's time you were walkin'."

"He said that, did he?" Uncle Caully grinned. "I'll be there, honey, if I got to get down on my hands and drag my good leg behind me."

Aunt Etta put her hand on Caully's shoulder. "He's doin' okay," she said. "I'm thinkin' he'll be walkin' by Christmas Eve."

That afternoon Mrs. Tate finished another load of wash for the mine foreman's wife. She stacked the pieces neatly in the laundry basket. "Bea! April Ruth! You girls carry the wash to the Wallers. The basket's full to the top, and you watch your step. Mr. Waller's got a Sunday-pressed shirt on top."

Bea looked slowly up from the present she was wrapping, and Jed decided it must be for Preston Harvey, the way she was working it over. "I'll carry it, but I'm goin' after dark. I just ain't walkin' up that road with it so's folks can see."

Mrs. Tate looked at her oldest daughter. "What's so wrong in folks seein', Bea? Think there's a person in Tin Creek don't know the problems we're havin' with Caully's operation to pay?"

"Mr. Waller got to have that shirt this afternoon?" Bea asked.

"No, not that I heard . . ."

"Then I'm goin' after dark," Bea insisted, and Mrs. Tate said nothing more.

So Christmas came, and it was the way Christmas Day should be—cold, with a thin crust of snow on the ground and more to come. The miners didn't strike because the company said they'd see to the rock-dusting. So the pay kept coming, and there was bacon and coffee Christmas morning.

Uncle Caully hobbled about on his crutches and even made it into the Tates' house without help. There was a tree all decorated with cardboard stars and angels, strings of popcorn, and some red foil milk-bottle caps that whirled around and around when anybody opened the front door.

"Merry Christmas!" April Ruth yelped, and thrust some presents on Uncle Caully's lap, and the front room was alive with the usual Christmas hubbub. Father whistled over the work

98

socks Jed had given him—extra thick, the way he liked them, he said—and Mother and Aunt Etta compared their lipsticks and powder and prettied up before the afternoon church service. Bea wore her bracelet over her sweater sleeve where it was sure to be seen, and Uncle Cauly filled his pipe with the favorite tobacco that Jed had finally purchased for him at Parsons'.

It was April Ruth who liked her present the most. "Two pieces sheet music! Oh, Jed, where'd you get 'em? 'April Showers'—my favorite! Ma, did you see what he bought me? *Jed* did. He picked 'em out himself!"

Jed got the knife he wanted—from Bea and April Ruth together—a real jackknife with a bone handle and blade as sharp as a razor. There were clothes from his parents and aunt and uncle, of course, but the knife was what he really wanted, and Jed was happy.

Mrs. Tate put the smoked ham in the oven just before the church service. Mr. Morgan, the circuit minister, had been to Grossen's Point in the morning and was holding services in Tin Creek at four. Except for two services on Christmas, he preached at Tin Creek the first and third Sundays of every month. The family put on the best clothes they had, and Jed discovered that his mother had put a new pair of cardboard insoles in his shoes to keep the snow out of the holes underneath.

They got into Uncle Caully's pickup truck, with Etta driving, and went to church. There was evergreen at each of the windows, a red ribbon tied on each branch. Red and green candles decorated the altar, and there was a small manger scene in front from Christmases past.

"Merry Christmas, Caully—Merry Christmas, Etta," people said as they grouped around the door of the church, and the snowflakes fell faster. "Good to see you, Caully. Merry Christmas, Sam—Lona. How's it going? Hi, Jed—Bea—April Ruth. Merry Christmas!"

But the Tates and the Mileses didn't greet each other. Jed and Tommy exchanged grins, and Tommy held up a pocket flashlight to show what he'd received for Christmas, but the adults looked the other way.

"Sam," Mother whispered as they sat down in a pew. "Couldn't we just say 'Merry Christmas' to 'em? Would it hurt so bad?"

Big Tate neither moved nor answered, but kept his eyes fixed on the pulpit. A trio of ladies up front began singing "Joy to the World," and church had begun.

Miss Singer had not gone back to Ohio for Christmas. Some said she didn't have any family to go to, and Jed decided maybe that was why she had come to Tin Creek in the first place. She had a room at the Morgans', and now she sat beside the minister's wife. Christmas was no time to be alone.

After the service, she came over to see Jed's family. She wore a pretty, red coat with a corsage of bells on the lapel, and her hair was combed down long over her shoulders instead of pulled back, as it was in the classroom.

"Merry Christmas, Jed," she said. "We had some snow after all, didn't we?"

Jed grinned.

"How are you, Mrs. Tate—Mr. Tate?" she inquired, shaking their hands, and they answered pleasantly.

"Jed made me the loveliest paperweight," Miss Singer went on. "Did he show it to you? I'd no idea what he could do with a piece of wood. Are you working on anything else, Jed?"

"Nothin' right now," he said.

At that moment, Uncle Caully started to get up from the pew, lost his balance, and sat back down again, struggling with his crutches.

It was the first time Miss Singer had noticed his missing leg.

"Oh, Jed! There's been an accident, hasn't there? I'm so sorry! I hadn't heard!"

"It was an operation," Jed explained, "but

101

Uncle Caully's doin' real good. You should see how he gets around."

"Well, it's wonderful the things doctors can do now," Miss Singer went on. "I have a friend with an artificial arm, and she can pick up even the smallest objects with her hand. It's just amazing."

There was silence. Aunt Etta opened and closed her purse.

"Well, I reckon I can get by on the leg I got left," Uncle Caully said finally. "Never needed nothin' artificial before and don't want to start now."

Miss Singer blinked. "I just meant it's not necessary to go about on crutches when you can walk without support. Why, they say you can even dance on an artificial leg!"

Uncle Caully grasped the back of the pew in front of him and stood up. "I don't expect to do much dancin', ma'am," he said, unsmiling, and went clumping back up the aisle. But Aunt Etta did not follow.

She stood there in her brown hat with her short, gray hair curling up under the brim, her brown suit decorated in front with a gold-colored wreath pin that Lona Tate had given her seven Christmases ago, her eyes small and dark in her full, white face, and her thin lips set in a severe line.

102

"How Mr. Tate gets about is no concern of yours, Miss Singer," said Aunt Etta, her words sharp as the rap of a hammer. "Some folks is sensitive about discussin' personal things, you know."

"Oh, but there's no need to be sensitive about it," Miss Singer said earnestly trying desperately to remedy her error and only making it worse. "Not in this day and age!"

Aunt Etta stood still, unmoving and unsmiling. "It's not just a day and age, young lady. It's a village and it's people. We got feelings here, Miss Singer. And they go against folks pushin' new legs on us what we don't want, and sendin' kids home from school when they can't be handled."

If there was ever a time Jed wanted to disappear, it was now. Not only did Miss Singer know now how Jed's parents had felt about her sending him home that day, but she knew that they had told it around Tin Creek as well. But it was Miss Singer's cheeks that were flaming now—almost matching the red of her coat.

"I'm sorry," she said.

"People's got to be treated like people," Aunt Etta said again.

"I'm sorry." Embarrassed and confused, Miss Singer turned and walked quickly back to the minister's wife.

"She was tryin', Aunt Etta," Jed said. "She was tryin' to make it up."

"She's a lot of learnin' to do herself, that girl," Aunt Etta said, watching her go. "They send 'em from the cities before they know what the country's all about. All she learnt about life, she's learnt from a book, and there ain't no praise in that."

Jed tried to figure it out on the way home. Miss Singer had been rude, no doubt about it. You just didn't say things like that to people when you'd hardly met them. You didn't say things like that to Uncle Caully, in fact, no matter how long you'd known him. You got sensitive to other people when you grew up in Tin Creek. You knew what was going to make them angry or sad even before you said it, and then, of course, you didn't say it. But couldn't Aunt Etta have softened it a little?

There was ham and gravy and hot biscuits for dinner. There was canned corn and tomatoes and lima beans from Aunt Etta's garden, and boiled onions in cream sauce. There were fried potatoes and fried apples with sausage, chess pie, all crunchy with brown sugar crusted on the top, and a huge chocolate cake Aunt Etta had made. Jed had never eaten such a dinner in his life, so he ate slowly, stuffing it in, knowing that the food would rarely again be this good, probably not before the next Christmas, if then.

However Uncle Caully felt about the teacher's remarks, he didn't hold onto it now. It was a time to be merry, and that he was.

"All we need now is Uncle Caully playin' his saw!" April Ruth burbled after dinner, and stopped instantly, horrified at what she'd said.

But Caully laughed. "Wouldn't sound so good braced between a leg and a crutch, gal. I'll take up the harmonica and see if I can't learn 'Silent Night' real pretty by next Christmas."

Preston Hardy came over to see Bea after dinner, of course, and even managed to notice the rest of the family. He actually sat down in the front room for a few minutes and talked to Pa and Uncle Caully before he and Bea went off through the snow, laughing at the flakes which occasionally floated down past their noses, trying to catch them with their tongues. Jed couldn't understand how anybody could be so silly around someone he really liked. It seemed like the fonder Bea and Preston got of each other, the sillier they became.

"They're gettin' serious, Lona," Aunt Etta said, watching them go. "Bea's gonna make herself a Hardy come summer. Mark my words. She'll be a June bride sure as I'm standin' by this window."

Mrs. Tate sighed. "Well, I can think of worse matches. Preston's a decent sort. Long's she finishes the school year out, I'll not complain. But she's not said a word about marryin' to me."

"They never do," said Etta. "Never do."

After Uncle Caully and Aunt Etta went home, Big Tate stretched out on the couch and Mother sat down beside him, rubbing his big back with her small hands, pushing hard against his ribs, making him grunt. Jed liked when this happened. It meant the feelings were especially good between them.

"It's been a good day," Mother said, keeping her arms straight and squeezing the big muscles on his back. "Sometimes . . . when you're in the mines . . . and . . . we've had words that mornin', you and I . . . I worry if somethin' should happen that day, and the last you'd remember of me was my hollerin'."

Big Tate smiled and put one big hand on her knee.

"No, Lona, it's not that way," he said. "When I think on us, I remember the whole things, and fightin's only a part. You can't live each day like it's goin' to be the last and sayin' only what you'd say if it were. We know how we feel about each other, and quick words don't change that any."

Christmas was over, but an excitement still

106

hung around Jed that no one but his mother understood. She didn't mention it, though, until one day, the second week of January, when Jed came home from school.

"There's a letter, Jed," she called from the kitchen. "It's on the radio."

Jed's feet seemed to freeze to the floor. He stared at the white envelope, his heart pounding like a jackhammer. It didn't feel like there were any dollar bills! Then he remembered that prize money would certainly come by check, and his hands actually trembled. For weeks he had thought daily of the contest, mulling over the various possibilities, and now that the letter had come, he was almost afraid to open it.

He put down his school books and picked up the envelope, examining it line by line.

"Jed Jefferson Tate," it read, in typewriting, like he was somebody important. "Old Hollow Road. Tin Creek, West Virginia." His heart began to pound again as his eyes shifted to the upper left corner. *Horace Bookstore*, it read, and he tore the envelope open.

For a moment his eyes rested on the first line. It was all he needed to know. Mechanically he skimmed the page:

Dear Contributor:
    We are sorry to inform you that

your entry did not win an award in our contest. We appreciate your effort and your interest and hope that you will submit another contribution next year. You may pick up your entry at our store any time during business hours. Again, thank you for helping make our contest a good one.

Morgantown Arts Society

For a moment, Jed felt as though he couldn't breathe, as though his lungs simply would not move. Then he dropped limply down on the cot and lay motionless, his stomach sick.

"Jed?" said his mother from the doorway, and waited. Finally she came on into the room. "It's about the contest, ain't it?"

There was no answer.

"I'm sorry, Jed," she said, her voice tender. "I'm really sorry."

Jed still could not answer, and finally she left him alone. He closed his eyes tightly. He was too hurt to move—too hurt to think. Maybe his father was right. Maybe all his hands would ever do was dig the coal, deep down below Tin Creek, down under the mountain.

Chapter Six

When Jed woke up, remembering, he lay as though he were dead, hating himself. To have entered the contest at all was dumb enough, but to have honestly expected a prize—three, in fact—was stupidity beyond belief. How they must have laughed at his carvings! How they must have gaped and stared and smirked at the backwoodsy little statues that probably looked like mud pies beside the modern, graceful lines of the contemporary sculpture—the form-less people without faces and the three-legged horses and the wire abstracts which Jed could not understand.

He winced with the pain of remembering. If only he hadn't missed the bus coming back, Mother would never have known. He hated that Mother knew. He hated himself and Tin Creek and all the dreams that were born here in this horrible backwater mudhole.

But Mrs. Tate kept her knowing to herself. At breakfast, she served Jed's grits on a warmed plate, a sort of special way she had of showing affection. But Jed wanted no sympathy. He was mad at everything there was in Tin Creek and took it out on April Ruth, who was humming "White Christmas" as she buttoned her dress.

"Will you shut up?" Jed said, spitting out the words. "It's two weeks after Christmas and you're still singin' it. I wish I'd never give you the music, the way you carry on."

"So what's it to you?" April Ruth retorted. "Nobody was askin' you to join in, the voice you've got!"

"I got to listen, that's what! Sounds like a sick hen! Only thing worse than your singin' is your piano playin'."

It hurt April Ruth more than she cared to admit, and she didn't answer.

"Jed!" Mother said, and nothing more.

110

Jed leaped up and grabbed his school books, taking his jacket with him.

"Okay, then, let her sing the roof off. But I don't have to listen!" He started out for school early, zipping his jacket on the way, seething at everything, knowing he'd been unfair to April Ruth, but not caring.

He hung around outside the school, refusing to go in, even though Miss Singer was already there. When Tommy arrived, the two went in together and threw spitballs back and forth every time Miss Singer had her back to the class.

He did everything he could think of to be contrary. He recited the alphabet while the others were saying the pledge to the flag and refused to sing the opening song at all. Later, during arithmetic, Tommy was sent to the board to work out the cost of 100 pencils at 29¢ per dozen at a discount of 10% for items over 50. Jed's mind wandered. 100 pencils . . . $100, the first prize. And all he was going to do with it! What a sap he was! What an idiot! What things he wouldn't have bought, though!

He hated himself even more because he was thinking about it—thinking about the prize money as though he'd even had a chance at it. He took his pencil and cut a deep line down the center of his desk with the lead and right on across his left hand, as though he were cutting it off.

"Don't mark the desks, please." Miss Singer was looking at him. Jed put down his pencil and sat glaring at the pages in his arithmetic book. "Do you have the answer to the first problem, Jed?"

"No."

Miss Singer waited. "Have you been working on it?"

"No."

"Will you stop by my desk at recess, please?" she said, and turned her attention to Tommy.

Jed walked cockily up to the big desk at recess. He stood twirling his pencil around and around his fingers like a baton, avoiding the teacher's face. Miss Singer waited until the other children were outside.

"What is it, Jed?" she asked.

Jed shrugged. "What you mean?"

"I mean what's bothering you?"

"Nothin'." His voice squeaked a little.

"Sure?"

There was no answer. The squeak in his voice betrayed him, and he didn't trust himself to say anything more.

"You're just not acting yourself for some

reason, Jed. Anything wrong at home? Anything you want to tell me about?"

The nosy teacher again—as though anybody would tell her. As though she could just ask right out and expect you to answer.

"Nothin' that's your concern," he said, amazed at his own rudeness and at once embarrassed.

Miss Singer drew back instantly. "I didn't mean to pry," she apologized. "If there's . . . there's anything I can do to help, I'll be glad to listen. Meanwhile . . ." she began rustling the arithmetic papers defensively, "I'll expect better behavior of you in the classroom. That's all."

Jed went outside and leaned against the building, eyes on the ground. Why hate her? She wasn't part of the local scenery. She didn't have creek water in her blood. She hadn't been raised on bread and lard and a ton of homemade apple butter. He'd predicted she'd be gone when he got back from Christmas vacation, but she wasn't. Stupid woman.

It was a cold Friday evening. The first snow had gone, leaving the ground frozen and gray. The mountain, hidden no longer by trees, stood out huge and stark against the night sky.

113

The grown-ups in the village had gone to a community meeting at the church, and the younger ones hung about in front of Parsons' store, wishing it were warmer. April Ruth was copying down the notes of a song on some music paper she'd bought in Morgantown, and Bea was primping for her date with Preston. Jed found them both disgusting, and went on up the hill to Parsons' to see if Tommy were there.

Jolly was sitting on a pear box outside the store, eating a sack of jelly beans, and Tommy was standing across the road throwing sticks at her bare legs.

"Stop it, Tommy! You'll hit the window!" Jolly squealed.

"Go inside if you don't like it," Tommy said, tossing again.

"I've got a right to sit outside my own house if I want to," Jolly protested, drawing her legs up under her.

"Yeah, you're glued to that box, all right," Tommy laughed. "I dare you to get away from the window. Go on—walk on up the road. I dare you."

It was unfair, of course—picking on Jolly. But Jed didn't care.

"Oh, let her alone," he said. "Any nerve she's got's in her feet. That's why she's always runnin'."

"I got as much nerve as you," said Jolly, picking out a black jelly bean and flinging it at Jed.

Jed caught it and popped it in his mouth. "Yeah. I'll bet. Bet you'd never do what Tommy and I are gonna do."

"What?" Jolly asked.

Tommy looked over. He didn't know either, and Jed knew he'd have to make something up fast. He thought of all the trouble he could get into back home, with his parents away at the meeting. Then he thought of Bea.

"Tommy and me are gonna hide in the back of Preston Hardy's car when he comes for Bea, and we're gonna see where they go. That's what."

Tommy's eyes opened wide, a grin spread across his face.

"Huh!" said Jolly. "I wouldn't be afraid to do that."

"Okay," said Jed. "Come on."

Jolly stood up and started down the hill toward Jed's.

Jed's heart began to pound as he and Tommy walked behind her. He'd said it, and now he had to follow through. When they got to the house, Preston Hardy's car was already there, and Preston was inside with Bea. Jed could see his sister fussing with her hair in

115

front of the window. She had it piled up high on top of her head and was trying to put on a little white hat.

Tommy was looking in the car. "There's not room for more'n two down there," he said, pointing to the floor of the back seat. "Jolly tries to get in too, they'll see her."

Jed felt enormously relieved. It had been a dumb idea.

"So?" said Jolly, stuffing the last of the jelly beans in her mouth. "I'll get in the trunk."

Jed stared at her.

"Go ahead before they come out," Jolly said. "Put me in the trunk."

Jed walked woodenly around the car and opened the trunk. Jolly crawled in beside an old suitcase and crouched down. "Okay," she said. "See if the lid will close."

Jed tried. "You'll have to scrunch down further," he said, and Jolly flattened out. This time the lid shut tight.

"Hey, this is great!" Tommy said. "This is really wild! We better get in before they come out."

Jed opened the door on the left side and they crawled in the back, pulling the door shut behind them. They crouched down as flat as they could. Tommy giggled. "Hey, Jolly, you okay?"

"All set back here!" came Jolly's muffled voice from the trunk.

Jed heard the front door of the house slam and Bea's voice as she and Preston came across the yard to the road. He could feel his heart pounding against his knees. Of all the stupid ideas! Bea and Preston never went anywhere. They just rode around and around the cemetery, or stopped and necked. But going or stopping, he and Jolly and Tommy would have to be quiet and couldn't even stretch their legs, and Bea wouldn't get home for three or four hours. It was the dumbest thing he'd ever done in his life—next to entering the contest.

The door on the right side opened and something big was hoisted onto the back seat. Then Bea got in front, and the door slammed again. Jed waited, wondering. Slowly his eyes turned to the object on the back seat. In the darkness, he could just make out Bea's canvas suitcase. *Now* what . . .

The left door opened and Preston Hardy slid inside. A moment later Bea was in his arms and cooing. "Oh, Pres, we did it! We did it! And nobody saw! April didn't even notice!"

Jed's eyes opened wide. Notice what?

"We'd better get on," said Preston, kissing her. He started the car, gunning the motor the way he always did, and the car jerked away

117

from the ditch and went groaning up the dirt road, past Parsons' and the nickel-and-dime, turning left at the schoolhouse, and heading east.

Jed and Tommy didn't dare whisper. They were packed in so tightly that their ears rubbed each other's, and they hugged the floor, trying to roll with the car so they wouldn't make any noisy bumps. Jed thought of Jolly in the trunk and hoped the lid was closed tight. What if she fell out and a truck ran over her?

Bea was cooing again. "I can't believe it, Pres! The biggest moment of my life! I was sure someone would notice, the way I was takin' so much time gettin' dressed...."

"You look real purty, Bea ..."

"The hat, too? It's Ma's, but she won't miss it till summer. I'll give it to her after I tell her."

"What you think she'll say?"

"About the hat?"

" 'Bout our gettin' married."

Jed's heart stood still. Getting married! Bea and Preston were getting *married!* Tonight! And nobody knew except him and Tommy and Jolly. Oh, it was great! It was wild! It was awful and terrifying!

He felt Tommy poking him in the side and

he poked back. Fairmont! That must be where they were going!

Preston turned on the radio, and he and Bea went on cooing, but Jed could hardly hear what they were saying. Only a few words here and there . . .

"Does your cousin know we're comin'? . . . job in Morgantown . . . selling shoes . . . good bonus if you work at it. . . ."

Jed's legs were getting numb, but he was too excited to care. What should he do when they got there? Try to stop the wedding? They'd kill him. Bea would absolutely choke him. Besides, if he stopped it this time, they'd just run off again and do it another time. Why not let Preston have her?

He wiggled his toes to keep them from getting numb. Just when he thought he couldn't take it any longer, the car slowed down and stopped. Bea gave a little giggle. "I'm sorta scared, Pres."

"Of me or the preacher?" Preston said laughing, but he sounded a little scared too. "Come on."

Preston got out on his side and went around to help Bea. The door closed and Bea and Preston started up the steps of a large, white frame house.

"My gosh!" Tommy cried, slowly rising up. "Jed! They're gettin' married!"

Jed peered out the window at the sign on the front lawn. "Justice of the Peace. Notary Public. Walk in."

Just as Bea and Preston reached the front door, a man came out with his hat on. He talked to them for a minute, looked at his watch, and finally went back inside with them.

Jed scrambled out of the car. "Come on!"

They tiptoed up the steps to the long porch and over to the window. The justice took off his hat and set it on his desk. His wife came in from the kitchen, wiping her hands on her apron and smiling. The man took a book off the shelf. He put Bea's hand on top of the book and Preston's hand on top of hers. He said a few words, closed his eyes and said a few more. After that, he turned to Preston and said something. Then he closed his mouth and Preston opened his. The same thing happened with Bea. Finally the man put his hand on top of Preston's, which was on top of Bea's, which was on top of the book, and said something else. And then—*then*, Preston turned Bea around and kissed her right there! Jed could hardly watch. It was awful. Preston was crazy, that's what— to do a thing like that right out in front of everybody.

Then the man opened his desk and took out a piece of paper, and everybody signed their names, even the woman in the apron. Then the woman took the flowers out of the vase on the desk and gave them to Bea, and Preston paid the justice, and before Jed and Tommy knew it, the front door was opening. They flattened themselves against the wall.

The justice had his hat on again and went hurrying out to his own car and drove away. Bea and Preston went down the walk very slowly with their arms around each other and stopped on the sidewalk to kiss again.

Jed's heart leaped up in his mouth. Jolly!

Bea was already in the car, and Preston was just getting in when Jed yelled.

"Jolly!" He sprang down the steps and went racing out to the car with Tommy behind him.

Bea jerked around and stared at them through the car window, her face turning white. Preston was struck dumb.

"You got to let her out," Jed gasped, leaning against the car.

"You're crazy, kid," said Preston. "I just married her."

Jed shook his head, panting. "No. The one in the trunk."

Bea opened the door and got out, and the

justice's wife came out on the porch to stare.

"Jed, what you doing here? What you talkin' about?"

"You got to let her out," Jed said again. "Jolly."

Preston's mouth fell open. He reeled around to the trunk and opened it. Jolly was curled up in one corner, with one leg tucked under her and the other curled back against the roof of the trunk. She had to tug on her legs with her hands to make them move, and finally, she rolled out onto the street and stood up, grimy from the dust of the trunk.

"See?" she said triumphantly to Jed. "I did it! And I didn't make no noise, neither!"

Bea turned on Jed. "Jed Jefferson Tate, you're hateful! *Hateful!* You three kids was in the car all this time . . . !" She put her face on Preston's shoulder and started to cry.

Preston was angry now. "We're goin' right on to Morgantown, honey, and the kids'll have to get back best they can. It's like nothin' even happened."

"They'll tell," said Bea.

"Nothin' nobody can do now," Preston said, hugging her. "We're hitched. It's legal."

Bea quit sniffing and got back in the car. The car drove off, leaving Jed and his friends on the sidewalk.

The justice's wife came down the steps.

She didn't think it was funny either. "You'd better call someone to come get you," she said sternly. "I'll not be lettin' you walk all that way this time of night."

"Jolly's only one's got a phone," said Jed. He sat down on the steps beside Tommy.

Jolly walked to the front door, but turned around and grinned impishly. "I said I'd do it," she crowed, and went inside.

Within fifteen minutes after Jolly called home, all of Tin Creek knew that Bea and Preston Hardy had eloped. When Jed got home, Aunt Etta and Uncle Caully were in the front room waiting to hear the story again. Jed began to feel like a hero as he added all the details.

But April Ruth was furious. "I think it was a nasty thing to do," she said, resentful that Jed was present at her sister's wedding and she had missed it. "I think it's terrible when a girl can't even git married without a rat of a brother goin' along in the back seat."

But Mrs. Tate ignored her. "I guess I never really thought she'd git her diploma," she sighed. "I guess I always figured her and Preston was goin' to up and do it one of these days. But it would of been nice to have one member of the family graduate, wouldn't it?"

"Well," said Caully, "there's still April and

Jed. They've got good heads, both of 'em. I wouldn't give up yet."

Mrs. Tate smiled a little. "April Ruth'll have herself a beau before the year's up, I'll wager. And Jed . . . I don't know. I just don't know what will happen to that one."

"Where they goin' to live, Lona?" Aunt Etta asked, curious. "The gal hasn't got a pot or pan to her name."

Big Tate rested his big arms on his knees and shook his head. "Preston Hardy ain't never done anythin' in his life I know of 'cept drive that car around on the money his dad's makin' in the mines. It's a bad sign when a fella can't even earn his own gas."

"I heard 'em talkin' 'bout Morgantown," Jed volunteered, "about Preston's cousin and sellin' shoes."

Big Tate grunted again.

"He'll not be feedin' much of a family by sellin' shoes—few cents a pair. Bea'll beat the spring rains back—you wait and see."

"Bad news comes in barrels," said Aunt Etta finally. "A load at a time. When I heard the news about the post office yesterday, I said to myself, 'Etta, there's more on the way.' "

"What about the post office?" asked Jed, looking around. "Is that what the meeting was about tonight?"

124

"That's what it was about," said his father. "Tin Creek's not goin' to keep its post office 'less the volume of mail goes up. It'll come by way of Clarksburg."

"What's so bad about that?" asked Jed.

"I'll be out of a job, for one," said Aunt Etta, her faced creased with a worried frown, "and pretty soon there won't be a Tin Creek no more. Once a post office goes, a town goes with it. The farmers and miners won't stop by here anymore to get their mail, they'll quit tradin' at Parsons' and the other shops, and pretty soon we won't even be on the county map."

The only thing Jed knew about hard times was that they could always get worse. Of that he was sure.

Chapter Seven

The end of winter was even darker than the beginning. No more snow fell in Tin Creek, but the weather stayed cold. The few letters the family got from Bea in Morgantown hardly concealed her disappointment over the way her plans were working out and the way Preston's job was going. Aunt Etta continued to worry about the postal station and wondered how many months longer it would last. And on top of it all, the coal company hadn't kept its promise to rock-dust, and Sedge Miles was agitating again for the union to call a strike.

126

The harder the times, the more the villagers kept to themselves. If Miss Singer had found them cool before, they were impossible now. They avoided her on the road and ignored her if they found her shopping at Parsons'. So she took her meals with the minister's wife, paying her a small sum for board and keep, and spent her weekends on lonely hikes up to the head of the hollow where the creek began or on up the wooded craggy mountain. Except for church on Sunday, she never sat down with the men and women whose children she taught, and when she tried to edge her way into a small group standing outside the church on Sunday morning, the talking stopped, and polite, frozen faces turned in her direction.

Jed sensed her frustration in the classroom and knew instinctively what it was about. She was feeling as all the other city teachers did who came down from Ohio—teachers who discovered, after being here a year, that the villagers still hadn't let them in. And all the while, Jed worried that he might not get out—that somehow Tin Creek and the mines would swallow him up and that, except for an occasional trip to Morgantown, he was destined to live here all his life, a prisoner kept in, just as surely as Miss Singer was locked out.

He often stayed after school to clean blackboards. On one particular day, he was watching the dark streaks disappear as the slate dried, absorbed in his own thoughts, and Miss Singer was mending books at the corner bookshelf.

"What would you say, Jed, if I said I wasn't coming back next fall?" she ventured suddenly.

Jed felt all tight inside, angry that she'd asked.

"Didn't know you was plannin' on it," he said finally, sullenly.

She paused with a book in her hands. "You didn't expect me to?"

Jed shrugged. "Most of 'em don't."

He went on scrubbing down the blackboard. Somehow he wished he could say something nice, but something stopped him. He hated that she wanted so much to be a part of Tin Creek when he wanted so much to get away. And yet, he was glad she was here. He was glad there was some link with life beyond the mountain. But somehow he couldn't show it. The village never did.

"It's hard, you know," Miss Singer went on, as though she just had to talk with someone. "It's hard to live in a place month after month where everybody treats you like a barometer. The only thing they talk to me about is the weather." She was trying to be funny, but Jed's heart dropped down to his feet. He

128

didn't want her to talk about it. He really didn't. But she kept on. "What do you have to do in Tin Creek to . . . to be included? Be born here? Be related? Nobody expects me to come back. Is that why they don't let me in on what goes on?"

Jed turned quickly around. "There ain't no life here to speak of."

"Of course there's life here, Jed. There are all kinds of things going on. All kinds of problems. Why, there's a sanitation problem with the water that ought to concern everybody. There's no library and no funds for books, no doctor, no clinic . . . we could make Tin Creek such a beautiful little place, we really could, but nobody wants to listen."

That was it exactly. Miss Singer and all the other teachers saw all the things that weren't here—never had been. Nobody saw Tin Creek's attractions because it didn't have any. So why did they bother? Why did they want to turn it into something special? Who wanted to listen to all the things that Tin Creek wasn't? That's what the Ohio teachers could never understand. And they all went away saying they were through with the mountains. It was so easy for them. . . .

Brother Edgar Doon came to Tin Creek on a Saturday night, after a dusty poster in the window of Parsons' store had announced him for more than two months. He had a wife dressed all in white, like the county midwife, and a tall, pasty-faced daughter who sang solos in a high thin voice that didn't have any wiggle to it.

Brother Doon himself was a short man, a little on the fat side, with bright red cheeks and ears and neck, as though his collar were a little too tight. Mrs. Doon was fat, too, but taller than her husband, and her heavy legs stuck out chalky white beneath her white dress as she walked up and down the street during the day, shaking hands with everybody, laughing good-naturedly, and inviting everyone to come to the nightly Bible and prayer meetings, ending in a glorious revival the following Sunday.

Some nights Jed and Tommy slipped up to the prayer meeting at the church and hung around the door, watching the small crowd kneeling in a circle, their hands clasped together, praying for ailing sisters and brethren whose names the Doons read off with a detailed account of their suffering.

"Amen," said the men and women there on their knees at the end of each prayer. Though unwilling to unburden their own hearts to the evangelists, they were perfectly willing to listen to the trials and tribulations of kinfolk in other towns. The Doons' tall daughter would stand up and read the next name and affliction, and Mrs. Doon would clasp her hands over her large bosom and talk to God as if He were a cantankerous old king who had to be cajoled into healing one of his subjects. When everybody got up off their knees and sat down, the daughter and Brother Doon would sing a duet together, something called "Beyond the Sunset," because that's what the people wanted to hear most.

During the seven days that the Doons were in town, they stayed at the parsonage in the guest rooms next to Miss Singer's. Old Mr. Morgan, the circuit preacher, had gone to Clarksburg to have the cataracts removed from his eyes, and the Doons were a welcome replacement for a village whose only recreation was religion.

April Ruth began stopping by the parsonage after school, and Bonnie Doon, the daughter, helped her a little with her sheet music. She taught her what the sharps and flats meant at the beginning of the staff and gave her a leaflet of hymns to practice on, which Brother Doon said she could keep if she'd come to the revival Sunday night.

Sometimes, after school, when Mrs. Doon was walking through the village, popping her head in the small stores along the way and inviting folks to the revival, and Bonnie Doon was helping April with her piano, Brother Doon would walk up to the schoolhouse and talk to Miss Singer. The first time he came, Jed was cleaning the blackboard again, and Brother Doon started off by saying that Miss Singer had a fetching sadness about her that drew him to her, like a farmer feels when he finds a small bird with a broken wing, and he wondered if he could be of assistance in any way—just to talk with, if she liked.

Miss Singer tried to sound businesslike and polite. But her cheeks flushed red and she told Jed he could go any time he'd finished, which meant right away because Jed had finished ten minutes before and was just waiting to hear what the preacher had to say.

Later, horsing around in the woods with Tommy, he saw them walking slowly out across the gray meadow. Miss Singer had her arms folded over her chest as they walked, and whatever she was saying, Brother Doon was listening—the only one who ever had. Jed liked him instantly for that, if for no other reason.

Not many of the villagers went to the prayer meetings. The Slocums went and the Benning sisters, the Andersons, and the Pritch-

132

ards, but everyone planned to go to the revival on Sunday night. The Doons themselves promised a program of music—solos and duets and trios (with Mrs. Doon singing bass)—and this time even Brother Doon himself was dressed in a white suit the color of lamb's wool, and the three Doons looked like hospital attendants standing up by the pulpit.

The villagers came in sweaters and jackets, their hair combed and their boots polished. A number of the women wore black straw hats, but Miss Singer wore no hat at all. She sat by Mrs. Morgan in a pew near the front.

Over on the other side of the church, Tommy Miles and his father and mother sat in a pew near the back. The Parsonses were there and Mose Hardy too—Aunt Etta and Uncle Caully. Everyone in the village turned out for the revival, because it was one way to spend a winter evening and, if you wanted to skip the offering plate, it was free.

When the church was full, Brother Doon stood up and welcomed them all. His smile was big and friendly. It seemed to take over his whole face, and he said he was the happiest man on earth because he'd found God and God had found him, and you'll never know what a blessing that is, folks, till you try it. And then he said he knew everybody that was there had come because there was some dark blot way down in their hearts that only Jesus could see, and he hoped they'd go out of church that night cleansed and pure as the rain from a summer sky.

Then Bonnie and Mrs. Doon got up beside him, and they all sort of put their arms around each other and sang "Shall We Gather at the River?" They did another one, too—"Standing on the Promises"—and all the while Bonnie and her father were singing, "Stand-ing, stand-ing," Mrs. Doon in her deep voice, was singing, "Standing on the promises, standing on the promises."

After that the offering plate was passed around, and Brother Doon accepted it with his head down and his eyes closed.

"Folks," he said, "I know you don't have much money, and I know that some of you gave all you could tonight—gave till it hurt. I know you don't have it, but if you did have an extra hundred dollars to spare, how many of you would give it to the Lord's work?"

Almost everybody raised his hand except Big Tate. Big Tate rarely raised his hand about anything. He always said that volunteering was the first step to trouble.

"Ah, I knew you folks in Tin Creek had

hearts of gold, even if there wasn't any in your pockets," Brother Doon went on. "Well, I want to tell you something. I've been prayin' for you folks, and I've had a vision. I've had a vision that says you folks are goin' to get somethin' special you didn't expect—something extra. Maybe it'll be two dollars on your birthday. Maybe it'll be an insurance refund or a welfare payment or a raise in your salary you didn't expect. I don't know just when it'll come, and I don't know how much it'll be, but the Lord's sendin' it. It's on its way. And all I want you to do, folks, when it comes, is give half of it to the Lord. I know you said you'd give a hundred dollars if you had it, but the Lord knows how poor you are and He's willing to take only half. That's all. Give half to the Lord, just to show your appreciation, and keep half for yourselves. If it's two dollars, keep one and give the Lord one. If it's fifty dollars, keep twenty-five and give the Lord twenty-five."

While Brother Doon was talking, Mrs. Doon started down the rows handing out little envelopes with Brother Doon's name on it and a Charleston address.

"There you are, brothers and sisters," said her husband. "There's your 'Thank-you, God' envelope. All you do is put in half your blessing and send it to me for God's work, and I'll see that it goes for the Lord in a way that will sanctify His name forever, praise Jesus."

"Praise Jesus," said the Benning sisters.

There was another duet after that, between Bonnie Doon and her father, with Mrs. Doon at the piano, her wide frame spreading out over the piano bench, sort of tipping it back as she played.

Then Brother Doon looked real serious. He folded his hands together and fastened his eyes on the door at the rear, looking neither to the left nor to the right, and waited till Bonnie Doon sat down in a folding chair near the piano, where her mother was still playing very softly.

"It's about that black spot in your heart that I've come to Tin Creek," he said. "It's there. We've all of us got one. And only the good Lord himself can wash it out." His voice grew very solemn, but faster. "I know that some of you have said things to each other you wished you hadn't."

"Yes, yes," said the Benning sisters.

"I know that money's gone for gamblin' and drink and worse that should have gone for the Lord and His work. I know that some of you young women have put on dresses to emphasize the flesh, and that some of you young lads have sown your wild oats and await the reaper with a heavy heart."

"Yes, Lord," said somebody near the back.

"I know," he continued, clearing his throat, "that there's a feud of sorts goin' on between two families in this town that I won't name."

A low astonished gasp swept through the church, but Brother Doon didn't hear it.

"I know they haven't spoken a word they didn't need to, and that the sins of their fathers lives on in their hearts." The church was completely still.

"I know that there's going to be no peace in Tin Creek till these two men shake hands.

"Brothers and sisters," he said, raising his arms toward the roof, "I'm askin' you all to come forward, to come down to this altar and tell God about your sinnin'. I'm askin' you all to take the first step by standin' right up and comin' down here to tell the good Lord what a coward you've been and promise Him how you'll change. I'm askin' you all to forget your pride and come up here before your brothers and sisters and tell 'em there's a new day dawnin'. Who'll be the first to come, brothers —who'll be first?"

"Softly and tenderly, Jesus is calling," went the tune on the piano, and Bonnie was humming.

No one moved. No one even seemed to be breathing. The preacher had done the unpardonable—he'd mentioned a personal matter in public, a feud that remained unspoken even among people in the village. Brother Doon looked out over the silent congregation and went on.

"Courage, brothers—that's what it takes. You men know what courage is. You know what it takes to put on your lamps and go down in the mines. But it takes even more to face up to Jesus, folks. It takes even more to get down on your knees and open your heart, evil as it is. But Jesus is waitin', and He's callin' your name. Let one come and the others will follow. Let those two men with the feud on their hearts be the first to come, dear Jesus, let 'em be the first."

Big Tate stood up, turned, and strode up the aisle and outside. Several others did the same.

The piano played on, softer and softer, as more and more people began to leave. Brother Doon's mouth began to drop a bit at the corners and the red in his neck and ears began to spread to his cheeks. This was the climax of the

138

long week of prayer. This was what he'd been working on for seven days. Surely someone. . . .

The noise of creaking pews and feet on the aisles was louder now, drowning out the sound of the piano. Sedge Miles and his family got up, finally, even the Benning sisters, looking confused and disappointed. At last there was no one left but Miss Singer and Mrs. Morgan.

The piano playing stopped. Mrs. Doon and Bonnie sat staring at the man in the white suit who stood stiff and still in the front of the church, his back straight and his mouth set— a statue.

Jed slipped out the door and into the darkness. A moment later Miss Singer came out alone and started back to the parsonage, her head bent. The Doons were outsiders, and she knew what that was like.

Chapter Eight

The spring rains came, making the roads impassable, and all the schools closed for two weeks. "Mud vacation," the children always called it.

Perhaps it was a good time for Miss Singer to be by herself. Jed felt an empathy with this teacher from Ohio which he shared with no one else. For several days he sat on the back steps, watching the yard turn into a sea of mud under the pelting rain, sorting out his feelings about Miss Singer and Tin Creek and the evangelists

140

who came all the way from Charleston to bring The Word.

He tried carving sculptures like he'd seen in Morgantown—the long curvy-lined things with the strange twists and shapes. But he had no feel for them. He'd stare at his crude creations for a moment or two after he was finished, and then, in disgust, cut them into pieces and toss them out into the mud.

It rained for days on end. The men carried the mud into the mines with them, and it came back mixed with coal dust. Down at the foot of the hill, the new road was already flooded and the bus to Morgantown stopped coming. The villagers put two old rowboats in Uncle Caully's backyard to navigate around that end of the village, and to rescue the occasional stranger who tried to get through, not knowing any better, and found his car floating away. The water was already rising in Aunt Etta's backyard, and she'd stand out on her porch and wave away anybody she saw coming with a parcel to let him know that the mail truck couldn't get through. Everyone watched the skies for signs of a letup, but none came.

One afternoon the clouds grew blacker than ever, and the steady drizzle which had been falling since morning turned into a torrential cloudburst. With each successive moment, the rain grew heavier and heavier until the sound of falling water became almost a roar as it beat down on the tin roof and the tree trunks and the red clay.

The men were just coming up from the mines when word went out that Uncle Caully's house was flooding. The water had been lashing around the back step all morning, but when the cloudburst began, the water came seeping in under the door and up between the cracks in the floorboards.

By the time Jed and his father got there, Aunt Etta was sloshing around between the two rooms in her boots, piling rugs and magazines and table scarves into bushel baskets. The men picked the baskets up and started them up the hill, hand over hand, from one man to another, until they reached Jed's house, where they were piled on the front porch. Jolly and Tommy and Jed and the other children helped carry the smaller things, and they greeted each other merrily as they passed in knee-deep water at the bottom of the road, the rain streaming down their heads and hanging by droplets on their eyelashes.

Every year the flooding seemed to be worse. Jed could even remember when mud vacation used to be one week instead of two.

Always before, the water had risen up over the bank of Tin Creek and crawled across the yard to Uncle Caully's back door. But this was the first year it had come inside.

Uncle Caully hobbled helplessly around the rooms, stopping occasionally to look out the window and shake his head at the sky. Outside, the people kept coming, wanting to do what they could: children, all of them barefoot, women wrapped in oilcloth, men in hip boots.

The big furniture came out next, carried up the hill through the driving rain as the water inside the house got up to four inches, five, and then six. When Uncle Caully came out of the kitchen and saw the front room bare, with muddy water lapping against the freshly painted walls, his chin trembled, and he stood there weeping silently, without tears.

It was getting on toward evening when Tommy, investigating the bank, walked gingerly out on the swinging bridge, itself a foot under water, to survey the flood from there. Tin Creek had become a raging river, and Tommy stood knee-deep in water, clinging to the sides of the bridge as the water jostled it back and forth.

"Hey, Jed! Come look!" he yelled. "Big old alligator way down there by the new road."

Jed waded through the deep water, feeling his way along the bridge, and gingerly stepped onto it.

"Where?"

"Down there. See, right this side the road?"

"You're crazy. That's a board or somethin' got caught on the rocks."

"Looks like a alligator to me," said Tommy. "Look how it's movin'. . . ."

Jed squinted out over the rushing water and wondered if maybe it was an alligator.

At that moment, the bridge under their feet lurched violently forward, then back, and suddenly they felt the flat surface beneath them tipping up and up until they were both propelled sideways into the creek.

Jed went under. As the muddy water rushed past his ears, filling his nostrils, his legs scraped along the bottom, and he fought to stand up. The creek wasn't that deep. But he hadn't counted on the moving water. Each time he got a foot on the bottom and his head above the surface, the current would sweep him under again.

As he rose up once, he caught sight of Tommy trying to say something, his mouth open, his eyes huge and blurry. But then the creek closed in around his face, and the two

144

boys could only grasp at each other as they were pummeled about.

For a moment, they were lodged against the root of a tree sticking out in the creek, and as they gasped a lungful of air, Tommy choked, "Jed, we're gonna d . . . die!" And then they went under again, and Jed believed it.

Down near the road, however, the rocks in the creek had caught much of the debris and were forming a wall. As the water crashed into it and pushed back, the current slowed and Jed found he was able to swim and stay up. As he neared the rocks, he grasped hold with both hands and lifted himself up till his waist was above water. He lay there panting a moment, and then swung around to look for Tommy.

At first he thought Tommy was dead. He was bobbing around in the water face down, his arms flopping loosely as though he hadn't the strength to keep himself up any longer. Jed cried out and, reaching down, grabbed hold of his sleeve and pulled him up on the rocks. Tommy was belching water, so Jed shook him until he coughed and gagged and finally opened his eyes.

"Tommy, you okay?" Jed said, terrified.

Tommy gagged some more, and then sat weakly up on one arm, his eyes red from the water. Jed leaned back, relieved.

145

"I thought you were drownin'!"

"I was, practically," Tommy said. "I can't swim."

"What you mean you can't swim?"

"I mean I can't stay up, that's what."

Jed put his head in his arms and closed his eyes. All the years he'd known Tommy, and the jerk couldn't even swim! What were they supposed to do now?

"Hey, Jed! Look!"

Jed raised his head. Coming toward them was not one rowboat, but two.

Tommy rubbed again at his red eyes and stared. "Man!" he said. "A whole dang boat for each of us!"

"It's Pa!" said Jed.

"And the other's my pa," said Tommy.

The two boys sat side by side, watching curiously. There was already a crowd on the bank. It seemed so incredible that Jed could hardly believe it—two boats, one about twenty feet ahead of the other—each pretending the other wasn't there.

Sedge Miles' boat was drawing up, and a moment later it touched the rocks.

"Get in," he said to Tommy, and Tommy alone.

It was so ridiculous, so completely nutty that Jed wanted to laugh, but he knew better.

146

Tommy, however, could not contain himself, and as his father shoved off again, Tommy pulled off his wet T-shirt, waving it dramatically at Jed as they moved away from the rocks.

"Cut that out!" snapped Sedge, and Tommy stopped.

Moments later Jed's father reached the rocks and Jed got in. He sat on the seat behind his father, watching his pa's thick muscles bulging out beneath his wet shirt as he rowed. He felt overcome with embarrassment, rowing back in a separate boat. How long did a grudge go on, anyway? Would he and Tommy be expected to keep it going once they, too, went to work?

"I woulda' drowned if Tommy hadn't saved me," Jed began.

"It's lyin'," his father replied brusquely. " 'Twas the other way around, and you know it."

The boat scraped the bank, and Jed waded across the thick red mud to the back stoop.

For three days Aunt Etta and Uncle Caully stayed with the Tates until the muddy red water had receded from their house and began inching down the yard again to the creek bed.

The house at the foot of the hill was a

mess, of course. Thick mud, smelling of sulfur, and encrusted with sticks and rocks and other debris, stuck to the walls and the floor. But no one had to be asked to help. Just as the neighbors appeared when the house began to flood, so they came again on Saturday, with scrub buckets and mops.

By Sunday the house was dry and clean, and the moving in was like a celebration. Each family in Tin Creek brought a hot dish for Sunday dinner and a gift for the house as well. None of the gifts were new—all had been in use in other homes—and many were handmade: a large, yellow-and-green hooked rug, a wooden rocker with a handwoven thatched seat, seven jars of pear preserves and some watermelon pickles, a blue patchwork quilt, a small walnut magazine table, a large pottery vase and bowl, homemade bread, a rhubarb pie, and a large, woven-straw hamper with leather handles. All together, they looked like gifts for a bride.

Aunt Etta, who was usually silent only if she were ailing, was speechless. She stood in the kitchen doorway beside Caully, and several times she opened her mouth but nothing came out.

It was Uncle Caully who spoke. "Well,

148

folks," he said, putting one arm around Etta. "I guess I been prayin' for the wrong thing. All the time the water was risin' I was prayin', 'Lord, don't let it reach above the stoop.'" He stopped and scratched his head. "But next year I'll be prayin', 'Lord, let it rise quick and high, and may our good friends give us the same as last—especially the rhubarb pie.'"

There was much laughter and good feeling, and Aunt Etta urged everyone to help themselves to the potato salad that Jed's mother had made.

As if to apologize, the sun came out for the first time since mud vacation had begun, and the wet ground began to be spotted with dry cracked patches. The children went barefoot all day, and when the moving was over, the men sat on barrels outside Parsons' store and smoked cigars and talked about where the fish had been biting best the year before.

Neither Big Tate nor Sedge Miles was there, however, and Jed realized how far their grudge isolated them from community life. Jed and Tommy and April Ruth and Jolly played kick-the-can in a vacant lot behind the nickel-and-dime until dark, and reluctantly wandered home only because they were hungry.

Jed had just sat down in the kitchen when

the back door flew open and Aunt Etta, her face blotchy red with excitement, came rushing in, Uncle Caully hobbling behind her.

"Sam," she said, running on into the front room. "I've got an idea about the postal station." She sat down in the rocker and began rocking back and forth, her hands on her knees, as though she just couldn't sit still.

"What's up, Caully?" Big Tate asked, but Uncle Caully just grinned and nodded toward Etta. He knew better than to tell her story.

"We're going to keep the postal station and build up a business, too, that's what," said Aunt Etta.

Uncle Caully grinned even broader. "Oh, she's thought of everything," he said. "Wait'll you hear."

"If I know Etta, she'll start a train station and lay the tracks herself," said Jed's father.

"Not a train station," Etta laughed, amused. "A mail-order business, that's what. We'll increase the volume of mail and save the postal station the same time we're makin' money."

"You got to have somethin' to sell, Etta," Big Tate protested. "What have we got in Tin Creek anybody else would want to buy?"

Aunt Etta's eyes fairly gleamed. "Specialties," she said. "It came to me this afternoon

150

—just as clear as the sky. It was right after everybody went home. I looked around at my clean house, at all the things folks had brought, and I said to myself, these aren't just ordinary presents. Here's a rockin' chair you'd never find in a department store in Charleston—a quilt like you'd never see in Morgantown. I'm just bettin' there are folks outside in the big towns don't have time for makin' their own things that would pay to have us send 'em some, if they just knew how to go about gettin' it . . ."

"It sounds too easy, Etta," said Big Tate. "You got to advertise. You got to let people know. How you going to do that? It takes money . . ."

"I know, I know," said Aunt Etta. Her face was serious now, and Jed knew she didn't quite have an answer to that one. "First we got to find out how many folks is interested in makin' things for sellin'. Then we got to find out how much they're willin' to put in toward expenses. It'll take a while, that's certain, but once Tin Creek gets a reputation for handmade things—things you can't find just anywhere— letters will be comin' in every day. We'll put little ads in the big New York magazines, and pretty soon folks'll be orderin' things from far away as Maine."

"Etta, that head of yours never stops," said Jed's mother. "You're talkin' like Tin Creek could be the showplace of West Virginia...."

"And why not?" Etta demanded. "Why shouldn't Tin Creek be anythin' we want it to be?"

She had a dream, too, Jed decided. They never stopped coming, the dreams, even when a person was old.

Chapter Nine

Aunt Etta's idea caught on. If it had been Miss Singer's idea or the Doons' or the health inspector's or anybody else from the "outside," people would have listened politely, and said it was a fine idea, but they wouldn't have done anything more.

But because Aunt Etta was one of their own, born and raised in Tin Creek, married to a miner, and descended from a long line of mountain women, she was listened to with respect. And because it just so happened that she was the seventh child of a seventh child, some

153

thought her power almost supernatural, and she was considered a little wiser than most of the women in the hollow.

Now the talk of the village was what specialties each family should contribute. The old men who sat outside Parsons' and coughed and haggled over their endless business of swapping penknives, their lungs black from their many years in the mines, now haggled over who could build the best cane-back chair or the best birdhouse. Women, making the long trek down the hollow to Parsons' of a Friday, would stand around the counter with their bulging sacks of government commodities and argue over who should contribute the gooseberry jam and who would stick to quilts.

As the handmade items slowly began to pile up in Aunt Etta's front room, however, she became quickly aware that while some of the "specialties" were truly lovely, some were perfectly awful, and while a pressed flower picture might remind one of the flowers that grew wild on the hillsides, it was scarcely created with a sense of artistry, and would probably stay in Aunt Etta's front room forever since no tourist would buy it.

"Caully," she said one afternoon, just as Jed walked in with a plate of pork chops that his mother had sent down for their supper.

154

"It's come to mind that there's got to be some-one better at judgin' quality than me to say what goes for sale and what don't. We start off with a bunch of pressed flower pictures like those Thursday Sizemore sent down, and Tin Creek'll be known for sellin' junk. We'll be finished before we begin."

Jed looked at the crooked rows of red and yellow flowers that had been glued to a piece of cardboard and agreed. Anything as ugly as that ought to be hung in the sow pen, if at all.

"What's more," said Etta, taking the plat-ter from Jed and handing him a cornmeal cookie, "we need somebody that's got some connection with the world outside Tin Creek to help us advertise. I wouldn't even know how to start."

Uncle Caully was sitting at a mirror propped up against a flour sack on the table and was trimming his big, gray mustache with a straight razor. "You're right, Etta," he said. "Gotta have things what's decent to sell and gotta have people to sell 'em to. I sure ain't qualified to know."

"It's what I'm gettin' at," said Etta. She nodded for Jed to sit down and opened a pop for him. "I've been thinkin' on it, and the only person I know in Tin Creek who knows what things might sell is the schoolteacher."

Jed slowly lowered his pop bottle and stared at Aunt Etta. It pained her to say it. He could tell by the way she went on mashing the cooked turnips in the pan, thrusting the masher harder against the bottom and avoiding Jed's eyes.

Caully paused a moment with his razor, turned his head right and left as he looked at his mustache in the mirror. "Reckon she's the only one," he mused. "Question is, who's goin' to bell the cat? Ain't anyone in Tin Creek on good talkin' terms with her 'cept the pastor's wife, and she don't know nothin' 'bout business."

"I been thinkin' on that, too," said Etta, and her right hand beat harder. "Reckon you've said more to 'er than anybody else, so I'm guessin' you'll be the one to ask 'er."

The razor hung suspended between Caully's fingers as he turned to look at Etta. "*Me*, woman? Why, I ain't never said no more than a few words to her!"

"That's twice as much as anybody else has spoke," said Etta.

You can say that again, Jed was thinking, thrilled that Miss Singer was actually about to be needed.

Uncle Caully dropped the razor on the table and leaned hard on one elbow. "The schoolteacher'll say no without even hearin' me out."

"She'll listen 'cause she's been raised polite," said Etta.

"She'll say she's leavin' in June and never comin' back."

"Then ask her to help us through May."

"She'll tell me she ain't qualified to be judge of no homemade things."

"Tell her there ain't nobody else can do as well."

"I'd rather lose my one good leg than go see that teacher," said Caully grimly.

"I had a vision," said Etta, "that says she'll only say yes if you ask her."

Nobody knew, when Aunt Etta said she had a vision, if she meant an idea or a supernatural happening. And because she was the seventh child of a seventh child, nobody ever quite said no to Aunt Etta, Caully included, and Jed could hardly sleep that night wondering if Miss Singer would say yes.

Jed made his way to Aunt Etta's again with a letter to Bea. He had purposely scrawled out a few sentences and stuck them in an envelope so he'd have an excuse to go to the postal station and mail it. He had to know if Uncle Caully had asked Miss Singer yet. Most of all, he wanted to know if Miss Singer was still in Tin Creek. It would be three more days before mud vacation was over, and Jed hadn't seen his teacher since the night of the Doon revival. Unless someone warmed up to her soon, unless someone showed that they appreciated her coming up here and teaching in Tin Creek, she was likely to pack up her bags and leave for Ohio, and nobody would miss her till the children went back to school on Monday.

Aunt Etta was sorting mail in the postal station, and she took Jed's money and stuck a stamp on his envelope.

"Gettin' lonesome to see Bea again, aren't you?" she said.

"Not exactly," said Jed. He leaned against the wall and stuck his hands in his pockets, watching his aunt dividing the mail into piles. "Uh . . . Caully gone to see the teacher yet?"

"Not 'less he's up there now," Etta replied.

Jed walked across the road. Aunt Etta's protective goose hissed Jed away from the sleeping hound that lay spread on the ground in the warm spring sunshine. He crossed the yard and went on into the small house.

Uncle Caully was at the table playing solitaire.

"Jed!" he said, when he saw his nephew.

"Come sit down and play me a game of crazy eights, eh?"

Jed slid into a chair and watched his uncle shuffle the cards. "Naw, it's too nice a day for card playin'. I come over to get you out in the sunshine—get you some exercise."

"Gettin' my crutches in and out the doorway's all the exercise I need," said Caully, wiping one hand over his beard to make sure there weren't any crumbs from lunch in it.

"How come you ain't said nuthin' to the teacher yet?" Jed ventured.

Caully frowned. "You're gettin' to be like a naggy woman, Jed! I said I'd go see her in my own good time, didn't I? Ain't no big rush."

"What if she's fixin' to leave Tin Creek?"

"Then what I have to say won't stop 'er. No use rushin' things. Could be Etta'll change her mind, and then I won't have to go at all."

Jed shook his head in exasperation. "C'mon, Uncle Caully, let's go for a walk up to Parsons'—or somewhere. You ain't been out of the house, and Etta says you're like to grow roots."

"Okay, okay," said Caully. It was better than being nagged. He put on a sweater and hobbled out onto the porch, while Jed held the door open for him.

Somehow, Jed hoped to get his uncle a lot further than Parsons'. Somehow he hoped to get him up to Miss Singer's. Maybe, with Jed along, it wouldn't be so difficult for Uncle Caully to talk to her.

Caully was in no mood to go fast, however. He had to stop all along the way and inspect the buds on the trees. April Ruth saw him coming and ran out to show him the skirt she'd made over vacation. Then the Benning sisters came along and wanted an opinion on whether lightning striking an apple tree would injure the fruit, and Uncle Caully said there would probably be fruit but it was bound to do poorly.

Finally Jed said, "I'm goin' on up to the store and wait for you there, Uncle Caully," and when his uncle waved him on, Jed went up the road and into Parsons'. He bought a dime pop and sat down on a bag of cow feed to drink it, figuring what to do.

He'd hardly sat down before he saw two skinny legs in front of him, and he looked up to see Jolly standing there, eating a package of cupcakes. She stuck out her tongue and licked the yellow frosting off her upper lip. "Hi," she said.

"Hi, yourself," said Jed, and took another swallow of pop. He didn't know why he was so rude to her, he really didn't. It was just that she was so darn skinny.

She sat down on the feed sack across from him. "Half?" she asked Jed, and when he nodded, she broke the second cupcake in two, giving him the part with the most filling. He was sorry he'd been so rude.

"You heard Aunt Etta's latest idea?" he asked.

" 'Bout startin' a mail-order business?"

" 'Bout gettin' someone from the outside to help manage it."

"No. Haven't heard that part."

Jed looked toward the door to see if Uncle Caully were there yet. "She's tryin' to get Caully to go ask Miss Singer, and he hasn't got his nerve up yet to do it."

"Miss *Singer!* You reckon she might stay here if she was asked to do somethin' like that?"

"That's what I was hopin'. But Caully's not movin' less somebody puts dynamite under him. He's been sittin' around three days sayin' he'll do it. Aunt Etta had a vision says he's the only one what can get her to say yes."

He set the pop bottle on the floor and stood up. "Come on and I'll buy you a jaw-breaker," he said, and they went outside to the gumball machine.

"Pssst. Jed!" Jolly nudged him with her elbow. Jed looked up the road where she was pointing. Miss Singer was coming down from the parsonage with a market basket on her arm. And as Jed jerked his head the other way, he saw Caully coming up from the road below. Caully was a little closer than Miss Singer, but she was walking a little faster, and Jed figured that they should reach the door of Parsons' about the same time. What's more, Caully had seen the teacher and she had seen him, so he couldn't very well turn around and go back now.

"I reckon your aunt had a powerful true vision this time," said Jolly, wide-eyed. "Nothin' but a tornado goin' to stop 'em from bumpin' noses."

Somehow, however, Uncle Caully slowed down even more because Miss Singer reached the store before he did. She tried to look cheerful, but even her voice was timid.

"Hello, Jed . . . Jolly! The mud's almost gone, isn't it? Seems like the rains came all at once this year."

"Yes, ma'am," said Jed.

Caully was coming slowly up the slope, lagging to let the teacher get on inside. Miss Singer had just put out her hand to open the door when Jolly chirped suddenly, "Hello there, Caully. Sunshine's bringing everyone out, I reckon."

Miss Singer turned to greet Caully, who grew pink in the face as he tried to stare down Jolly.

"Hello, Mr. Tate," said Miss Singer. "She's right about the sunshine. I felt I just had to get out."

"Mornin'," said Caully, grimacing at Jolly.

But Jed knew that Jolly couldn't be stopped now. There was something about her eyes that told him Jolly was going to go on pushing till Uncle Caully walked right into it. Only a girl could get away with that.

Jolly avoided Uncle Caully's look. "Fancy the two of you almost bumpin' into each other," she burbled.

"We've both been stay-at-homes, is that it?" Miss Singer questioned.

Uncle Caully moved toward the door.

"Caully's been lookin' all over for you," Jolly went on.

"Oh?" Miss Singer looked at Jed's uncle.

Uncle Caully's face was bright red beneath his gray beard. His eyes fixed themselves on Jolly, his mouth open incredulously at her nerve, but Jolly rambled on: "Heard he had a question to ask you. Guess that's why he's so glad he run into you."

163

Jed watched Jolly with admiration. She had a lot of nerve, that girl! She just stood there smiling up at Caully like she hadn't the slightest idea what he was glaring about, and finally he snorted, "The young'uns! The young'uns! Why, if I had me two good legs, child, I'd . . . !"

Jed grabbed Jolly's arm and pulled her away. "C'mon, Jolly," he said, starting down the street. "Let's go find Tommy." They crossed the road and went behind the empty store, but there they stopped. "You did it! You *did* it!" Jed said. "You dumb, crazy, nervy girl! You did it!"

Jolly giggled appreciatively, and they stood peeking around the store, watching.

Uncle Caully had asked the teacher something, all right, because Miss Singer was sitting down on an upturned soda bottle case, listening intently.

Jed slid down to the ground, his back against the unpainted side of the empty store. "First time somebody besides Brother Doon and the minister's wife has said more'n five words to her."

"Folks what's born again are supposed to be kind to everybody," Jolly mused. "The way Tin Creek's been treatin' her, you'd think there weren't none of us been saved."

164

"How you go 'bout gettin' saved?" Jed wanted to know. "Get up in revival and confess, like Brother Doon asked us to?"

Jolly drew up her knees and wrapped her thin arms around them, her bony chin resting on an even bonier kneecap. "Takes a heap of courage to get up and repent of your sins in front of folks, but you still ain't born again. You got to be baptized first."

Jed sat thinking over this bit of knowledge about salvation. Jolly had been baptized last year in Tin Creek, before it got so acid. Now it burned your eyes so bad that this year's baptizing would have to be someplace else. The mine officials kept saying they were going to cover over the slag piles so the sulfur wouldn't ooze its way into the creeks and streams, but they never did.

Jolly knew a lot about religion that Jed didn't know.

"Is that the only way you can get saved?" he asked.

Jolly nodded. " 'Course, just gettin' baptized ain't no guarantee you're goin' to stay clean. I knew a girl went back on the Lord. She wouldn't clap her hands and she wouldn't shout in the church house—just sat in the back row with the sinners. I shout a lot. Whenever the Lord moves you, you shout."

"What if the Lord moves you to be quiet?" Jed wanted to know.

Jolly frowned at him. "You shout," she said again.

"How do you know for sure when you're born again?"

"You start feelin' God's power in you, that's what. Every once in a while I take a wormy spell. I mix water and turpentine and sugar, and drink that. The sugar makes the worms eat it, and the turpentine makes 'em stop biting on me. Well, right after my baptizing, I prayed about the worms but I forgot to drink the turpentine, and they stopped bitin' anyway. Now that's the kind of power. Besides, I know I belong to God 'cause I'm not cuttin' my hair. I'll just let it grow down to my ankles if He wills it. It's like the power of Samson. You got to believe the whole word of the Bible, or you don't believe none of it."

Across the street, Miss Singer was getting up off the bottle case and Uncle Caully was holding the door open for her. They went inside Parsons', and the screen door slammed. There wasn't anymore to see, and Jed felt it best not to get too close to Uncle Caully for awhile.

"I'm goin' home," he said, standing up.

"Etta'll be up with the news soon as she gets it from Caully."

"Promise you'll tell me what happens, Jed?" Jolly called after him.

"Promise," Jed said hurriedly, and suddenly he stopped and turned around. "Hey, skinny legs. Thanks! Thanks a lot!"

It did not take Aunt Etta long to rush up the hill and tell Jed's mother what had happened. Caully had put the question to Miss Singer, as Etta had told him to. And Miss Singer, after a good deal of thought and lip biting, had agreed to help out as best she could, providing Mr. Parsons and Etta would work along with her, and, of course, they said they would. Jed was jubilant.

Chapter Ten

On Saturday, half the men went to work in the mine for overtime. It was good when there was that much work. Sometimes the work was almost too good, with the coal coming out so fast that the men could work seven days a week if they wanted. Other times, when the coal came slow, they'd go down to four days a week or even three. Big Tate said his pa used to talk about going to work only two days every two weeks. It was hard to stay alive then, and once a man got into debt, he almost never got out.

It was almost eleven o'clock that morning when the rumor began—a whisper that seemed to travel about Tin Creek on the breeze, touching each household and bringing the women out into the street with their aprons on and their babies in their arms.

"The mine . . ." the gossip went from house to house. "Slate fell . . . men trapped . . ."

It didn't matter how many or who they were. It mattered that anything at all had happened to anybody down there in the dark of the earth. Like cattle stampeding at the sight of fire, the people went running up the hill to where the dirt road turned right, past the schoolhouse, past the meadow and the strip of woods, past the place where Tin Creek itself crossed the road at a footbridge, and then on up the hill to the barbed wire fence and the metal gate of Number 7.

The head man had come out of the tipple and was standing by the gate.

"It's only two of 'em that we know of still caught," he told the questioning women. "Six men in all were trapped and four got out. The rescue team's down there now, and I'll tell you everything I know soon as I hear it."

There was almost no sound except a faint moan from the women. Who were the four men out, and who were the two still trapped?

The man didn't know. Slate had fallen in one tunnel, he told them, but orders were to bring up all the men. The shaft was clear, and they were coming up as fast as the hoists could run, one cage going up while the other went down.

Jed's mother stood at the gate, her fingers holding so tightly to the wire, it made her knuckles white. A low murmur of talk went on around her, everybody telling what little he knew of this particular catastrophe:

"When slate falls, you don't hear it. It just comes down on you," one woman said.

"Could be ten men under there, for all he knows," another said, motioning toward the head man. "If all the men ain't up yet, how does he know how many's missin' and how many ain't?"

It was Etta talking now. "My man's been bundled up many times. Clay bank fell on him onct and almost killed 'im. But when the slate fell in the mine, that was the trick that done it. Turned his back and mangled his leg so he couldn't never go back down under. I'm just glad he's alive and able to do what he does."

The man hoist came to a stop and five miners got out. Jed couldn't make out who they were under the blackness of the coal dust. They walked into the lamp house and left their lights to be recharged and then came over to the women just as another load came up. Big Tate and Mose Hardy, Sedge Miles, and the oldest Parsons boy—all the men from Tin Creek were safe and accounted for, and the relief was so great that some of the women sat down on the road and breathed deep, like the strain of waiting made a pain in their chests.

Big Tate stayed inside the fence talking to the rescue crew as they brought up a miner just dug out. The man lay still and gray, strapped to a stretcher. When he'd been whisked into a car and rushed toward the General Hospital at Fairmont, Big Tate came over to Lona and the others. "Rescue crew says it's a man lives over in Barracksville was hurt. There's still one buried, and they don't know whether he's alive or not. A Clarksburg man, they think."

Jed stood at the gate and waited with the others, his throat feeling thick and his tongue heavy. It could have been anyone trapped down there. It could have been his father.

The women waited, sharing the few coats and jackets which some had brought. It didn't matter if your man was safe or not. As long as anyone was left down there, as long as it was anybody's man, they stayed it out—the silent vigil for the wife who probably hadn't even heard the news yet.

They brought him up an hour later, and he was dead. Silently the body was carried through the hushed crowd to a waiting ambulance. Silently, two miners left to tell his wife in Clarksburg that she was a widow.

Lona looked up at the sky and bit her lips. "To think the poor soul's probably standin' outside right now thinkin' what a lovely day it is, and a few minutes more she's goin' to be told the news, and the sun won't never again shine for her like it does now."

Another figure came striding toward the gate, through the group of miners and on out into the road. Sedge Miles had a look of fury on his face, and his mouth was pulled low at one side. "Now maybe the union will call a strike," he muttered. "We've waited long enough."

"Amen," said some of the women.

"We're with you, Sedge," said two of the miners by the gate.

Silently Jed walked home beside his father, Lona clinging to the other gray arm of her husband. The men would listen now, Jed knew, and underneath he was glad. Mother wouldn't worry so if the mine were made safer. And it looked like only a strike would make the company listen.

Not a miner went to work the following

Monday. They didn't need a strike to know that no man went to work the day after a man was killed. It was a mine tradition. It meant that the management would dock them their Christmas bonus, but it was the least you could do for a dead man, the least you could do to mourn his passing and protest the way he had died.

On Monday night, there was a union meeting, and the men voted yes, all but Big Tate. A strike was set for the nineteenth of May.

There was no school either on Monday. People sat around talking low, like at a funeral preaching. Jed didn't dare go to Tommy's house with Sedge stirred up like he was, and Tommy didn't dare go to Jed's so they ended up at Uncle Caully's and found him on the porch in the rocker. They had come out despite the pouring rain which made a gloomy day even gloomier.

"If it ain't two boys tryin' to die," said Caully as he watched them come across the yard.

"Won't hurt us none," said Jed, flopping down on the dry porch and shaking the water from his hair.

"One man dead's enough," Caully mused, his mind on the miner from Clarksburg. They sat silently awhile, each with his own thoughts.

"Somebody at the mine said you can't hear slate when it falls, Uncle Caully," Jed said finally. "That true?"

"Only the best ears can hear it, and then you got to hear when it's fixin' to fall, not after." Uncle Caully stretched out his good leg and folded his hands over his stomach, his gray beard touching his fingers. "A man's got to have good ears to be a miner. Some men just shouldn't be in the mines, that's all. Got to have good eyes—a good nose—just as important as the muscles in his back."

The sound of the rain grew louder on the tin roof of the porch. For a while Uncle Caully sat quietly, with a chaw of tobacco. Occasionally he spat a stream of dark bright juice sideways so expertly that it went directly off the porch without touching a thing.

"Used to be lots more dangerous than it is now, that's for sure. Used to be we did all kinds of hell-foolish things they don't allow 'em to do no more. Robbing the mines—that was one. We'd take out the pillars of coal we'd left standing to hold up the roof of the tunnel. We'd start way back the end of the tunnel and dig out the farthest pillars first, workin' our way out to the mouth of the hole, always listenin' and watchin' for the slightest crack to show that it was cavin' in. You'd lay on your side or get on your knees any way you could to get at the coal, and sometimes the roof'd give, and that's the way you'd find the men when they dug 'em out—on their knees, like they was prayin', with their probes in their hands. If I got to go, I used to tell Etta, I hope I go like that so the good Lord'll see I'm ready."

They sat motionless on the porch, watching the rain pelting down and listening to the rattle of pans from the kitchen as Aunt Etta worked at biscuits for dinner.

"Pa's never been as scared of the slate as the firedamp," Tommy ventured.

"Aye, it's worth bein' scared of," Uncle Caully agreed, and then—realizing he was fraternizing with the enemy, he added, "but the chokedamp'll do you in as quick as the explodin' kind. A man reaches a pocket of chokedamp, and he sinks to sleep as he lays at his work. Don't never know nothin' different." He shook his head. "There ain't no kind of trouble in the mine that's easy. When a man's buried in a cave-in, he's like as not left if the whole tunnel goes, 'cause he's buried as well as a company could be expected to arrange it. But if the rescue crew can get to where he's at, or if a part of him's stickin' out, the doc comes down and pumps opiates into him while the team digs him loose. I heard some awful screamin' in my day, you better believe. I worked the mines long before Big Tate ever got into 'em, and the stories I could tell would raise hair on the top of your tongue. Once there were eight men killed, and the force of the explosion was so great that some of the bodies got wedged between the shaft wall and the cage, and the rescue team had to cut them to pieces to get them out."

Again the silence, this time more awful than before.

"It's crazy, askin' men to go down riskin' their necks that way," Jed said hoarsely, restless. "I ain't never goin', Uncle Caully. I ain't never settin' foot under the mountain."

Uncle Caully looked neither to the left nor the right. "That's what all of us said, Jed, when we was your age. We all had ideas of doin' somethin' different. But as we growed up and seen the doors shuttin' all around us, and seen that the coal company was payin' higher'n most other places, we put on our lamps and went. That's how it was. Always will be, I reckon."

Beatrice and Preston came home to live. Bea's husband hadn't been able to earn enough selling shoes in Morgantown to support a wife and had decided to come back and go to work in the mines like his father.

176

They could have moved in with Mose up on the hill, but Beatrice was going to have a baby and wanted to be with her mother. She was sick half the time and couldn't cook, so she and Preston took April's room, and April Ruth had to sleep on a daybed in the kitchen.

"Just till the baby comes and Bea gets it nursin' good," Mrs. Tate told April. "House is just too small for two families livin' in, and Bea'll get along okay with Preston's pa once she can keep some food down her."

It was a situation nobody liked. Though there were two more people in the house, it was even quieter than it was before. Preston went to work reluctantly in the mornings, squint-eyed and sleepy, beside Big Tate, and came home exhausted and sullen. Big Tate began eating his meals silently instead of telling stories and laughing loudly as he used to do. April Ruth became whiny and quarrelsome at having to sleep in the kitchen, and snapped at Bea, who was in no condition to answer her back. Bea ate little, spending the rest of the evenings on the couch, half-asleep, with her feet propped up on a chair cushion. Mother went about tight-lipped, her eyes full of concern for Beatrice, and the worry lines in her forehead deepened as one more worry was added to the list.

It didn't bother Jed so much that they were living in. It bothered him that they'd had to come back at all. Here were two people who had tried to get out of Tin Creek and couldn't make it. What chance was there for himself— Jed Jefferson Tate? Each morning when he saw Preston leave for the mines, he saw himself, and felt as though the trap was closing in.

Chapter Eleven

There were two moods in the village. The coming strike in the mine, set for May 19, took some of the joy out of the mail-order business that Etta was organizing. But the bustle of the women as they went about collecting scraps of cloth from each other for the quilt making or trading recipes for cinnamon bread gave a lift to their spirits. The men, sitting on their back stoops, working on their birdhouses or rockers or whatever else they were going to sell, went determinedly about their work, as though desperately hammering their way out of the pall

179

of gloom which had settled down over the hollow.

"Them aprons is goin' to sell good, Thursday Mae," Aunt Etta would tell the young woman who brought another load over, "but I don't know 'bout them flower pictures. Maybe you ought to stick to aprons for a while till we see if there's any call for pictures."

Or she would say to one of the Green brothers, "I don't know, Daw. That sled you made ain't got the runners straight. Best you try somethin' out yourself before you try to sell it. What about them old lanterns back in your pa's barn? You reckon he'd be willin' to sell them as antiques?"

And every few days, when Miss Singer came down to see what else had been added to the growing accumulation of wares, she and Etta would look them over and decide what should go back and what should stay.

"I don't know about this one, Etta," Miss Singer would say. "Maybe we ought to try one or two and see how they go." Or, "Now these little pottery creamers are precious. I wish Cordie Jones could make a dozen of them."

At first, when Etta and Miss Singer and Mr. Parsons got together, Aunt Etta sort of referred to Miss Singer instead of speaking to her. At first she'd say, without even lifting her eyes, " 'Course, if the teacher thinks this one won't sell. . . ."

But this time Miss Singer waited her out. This time she did not blush or panic or apologize, but sat quietly in Aunt Etta's front room, speaking when she was spoken to, and in less than a week, Aunt Etta decided that the young thing from Ohio knew what she was talking about. It took only a few days to discover that Norma Singer knew a little about the business world outside of Tin Creek as well, and that if anybody was going to be able to advertise the things the villagers made, it was going to be the teacher.

And then one afternoon, Mr. Parsons drove up in his jeep and came running up the steps to the porch where Etta and Miss Singer were sorting out a box of potholders that Jed had just brought down from the Benning sisters.

"It's either good news or bad," said Etta simply, and there wasn't even time for her to have a vision. Jed saw Mr. Parsons' mouth stretch into a wide smile and knew right off it was good.

"We're a business," he gasped. "We're a real business now, and we got us a store."

"A store?" said Etta, her hands dangling off her lap.

"That's right. We're gonna up and move

all this here stuff to the empty store 'cross from
mine, and we're gonna have us a place where
tourists can drive from Morgantown on a Sunday and buy things direct if they want." He
sat down on the steps and leaned back against
a post as though the excitement were almost
too much for him, running one hand slowly
through his thinning red hair, his glasses
perched crookedly on his nose. "I just come
from Morgantown, and while I was at the hard-
ware store I come across Mr. Jacobson, what
owns the old store. I was tellin' him 'bout the
mail-order business, Etta, and he says we could
store the stuff in his old place if we wanted.
And then he says, 'Of course, if you want to fix
the place up, I'll let you have the first month
free, and after that you can rent it for a percent of the profits. Better'n having it sit empty,
with taxes to pay.' "

"I never!" said Etta. "Why, I never!"

"It's wonderful!" said Miss Singer. "Isn't
it great how things are working out, Jed? It's
as though Tin Creek were meant to be something bigger than it is." She stopped right
there, afraid she'd gone too far, but Mr. Parsons was already basking in the glory of it.

"Tin Creek Crafts—that's what we could
call it, Etta! If Caully ain't got nothin' better
to do, he could run the store for us."

182

It was an exciting time. Nobody knew what would happen for sure, but it was their store and everyone took a part in fixing it up. Women came down to plant flowers in the strip of dirt between the store and the dirt road. Uncle Caully stood on one leg, supported by his crutches, and painted the inside walls white. Sedge Miles put shutters on the four front windows and painted them red, and someone else decided that the front door should be yellow, and painted it one night when no one else was around. Some of the men got together and built display tables from rough lumber, and the women washed the windows and scrubbed the floor. It was, when it was finished, the nicest looking place in Tin Creek—the only nice place, in fact, and folks began to talk about fixing up other things, too.

Everyone was busy on his own special project, whether it was something homemade, or antique collecting, or helping out in another way to get things ready. For every item sold, the price would be divided between the person who made it, the store owner, and the mail-order business itself, to pay for the mailing and advertising.

Bea, now beginning to bulge with the size of her child, worked on a hooked rug during the day, and April Ruth helped her with it when she got home from school. Mrs. Tate sent Jed around to the neighbors to collect coffee and lard tins. Then she covered them with tinfoil and filled them with her molasses cookies. Every Saturday she would have a half dozen more cans to sell, and Jed would take them to the store and put them on a shelf near the front.

The month of April turned to May, and the opening of the Tin Creek Crafts Store was scheduled for the second Sunday. Miss Singer had been to Morgantown and tacked announcements of the opening on every community bulletin board she could find. She circulated them around the university, and left them in grocery stores, a book counter in the public library, and even in the foyer of the First Baptist Church. Small ads were placed in a New York newspaper and a national magazine.

The opening was a little more than a week off, and Jed was painting the front porch of the house. Everybody seemed to be doing something to brighten his own home, and Lona Tate decided that the porch should be blue, to go with the blue-gray shingles on the sides.

April Ruth was sitting on the steps, trying to hum the tune of a new song sheet she had bought at Parsons', when a big green car came slowly up the dirt road.

"Tourists already?" April asked, watching the car.

Jed dipped his brush in the paint again and started on the other post. "Maybe they got the announcements already and wanted to come before the things was all gone," he said. "We ought to put a sign down at Uncle Caully's pointin' up this way so's they'll know they're goin' right."

The car stopped, and the driver peered out, confused.

April Ruth stood up and walked barefoot across the yard. "Wantin' directions?" she asked.

The man smiled. "Looking for a family named Tate. There's one back at the junction, but a lady there said it wasn't the right one. Jed Jefferson Tate—that's who I want."

"He's my brother," April Ruth said, surprised. "Come on up the porch." She bounded back across the yard and sat down on the top step, one foot tucked beneath her, watching.

Jed put down his brush and wiped his hands on his jeans.

"Jed Tate?" the man asked, a rather portly gentleman in a dark brown suit, with wisps of dark hair to cover his balding head.

Jed nodded.

The man extended his hand. "I'm Mr. Horace, from the bookstore. You left some wood carvings with us last November for the contest, I believe."

Jed nodded again, his cheeks burning fiercely. Mr. Horace had told! He'd said it in front of April Ruth.

"He win somethin'?" April Ruth asked, and Jed wanted to die.

"I'm afraid not. Jed's carvings were in a much different style than the others we exhibited," the man said. "It was hard to compare them." He turned to Jed. "Since you didn't come to get them, I thought I'd return them myself. I think they're quite good, Jed— I really do—especially for a boy your age. It's a type of wood carving we don't see much of anymore, and I'd hate to see you give it up. Have you ever thought of selling these?"

Selling them? No. Jed had thought of winning one hundred dollars with them, and then of chopping them up and throwing them in Tin Creek, but never selling them.

"No? Well, think about it. I believe you should."

"Let's see 'em, Jed," April Ruth said, peering into the box which Mr. Horace was opening. Gingerly she lifted out the little white pine pig and turned it around in her hands.

"Jed did this?" She turned to him. "Honest, Jed? You made it yerself? I'll say it's good!" She turned quickly back to Mr. Horace. "We're openin' a crafts store next week. Jed could sell these there, couldn't he?"

"Absolutely. I saw an announcement of your crafts store and thought you might like these back for the opening, Jed."

Jed's mouth was still dry. If only April Ruth would shut up.

"H . . . how much do you reckon I should ask for them?" he said, figuring maybe fifty cents a piece and wondering if that was too much.

Mr. Horace thought it over. "I'd price them all differently, depending on how much work went into each and how good you think they are. The pig—about a dollar-fifty, I guess. . . ." Jed gasped. "The hay wagon, two— and the man and his fiddle, maybe four."

For a moment, Jed stood speechless.

"Do you have any other carvings?" the man asked.

None that were done, Jed told him, but a hundred ideas in his head.

"Work them up, Jed. I know some customers who ask for this sort of thing now and then, and I'll send them down here. You'll sell them all, I'm sure."

The fat man stood in the scrubby yard and chatted a little with April Ruth, but Jed didn't hear any of it. Then the man drove way, and April went screeching up the hill to Parsons', where Mother was shopping, to tell her about it.

By the time April Ruth came back with Mrs. Tate, Aunt Etta had come up from the bottom of the hill, and they all stood in the Tates' front yard, fingering the little wood carvings and staring at Jed.

Jed slipped around to the backyard and sat down on the stoop, puzzling over the jackknife as though seeing it for the first time. Was it true what the man said? Would people really pay to buy his things? Was this another dream to burst with all the rest? In his nervousness, he picked up a piece of white pine and began working on it without even thinking. Would they laugh at him behind his back? Would they say that he was trying to be better than all the other kids in Tin Creek—kids like Tommy who just accepted that he'd grow up and go into the mines? Would they say that carving figures out of wood wasted time—that it wasn't the same as making rockers or apple butter or a hooked rug? Rockers you could sit in, apple butter you could eat, rugs you could walk on, but carvings . . . ?

188

It was almost an hour later before he stopped to think about what he was carving. He looked at it, blinking. It was a goat—or would be, when he was finished—a little white goat like the one Tommy's father used to have —that ate up Tommy's new sweater right after Christmas one year and was sold to a man in Fairmont. It was half done already.

He was still staring at it when he was conscious of someone behind him, and looked up to see Big Tate in the doorway.

"I didn't know you was home," Jed said hastily.

"I didn't holler," his father said unsmiling, but his voice was gentle.

"I'll pump the water," Jed said. But still his father didn't move to let him pass.

"When'd you carve all them things yer Ma showed me, Jed?"

Jed's face flushed. "Last year," he mumbled. "Haven't done any of late—'cept this one."

"You kept 'em hid away?"

Jed didn't answer.

"How come you kept 'em hid?"

Jed shrugged.

"Got anythin' else hid away? Doin' anythin' else I don't know about?"

"No. Honest."

Big Tate reached out and took the half-finished goat, looking at it intently. "That true what the man said—you can git three-four dollars for each one?"

"He didn't say that. Maybe only one or two . . ."

Big Tate stared at the goat again, his face contorted with the effort of trying to understand. Finally he handed it back to Jed. "You're not countin' on it, are you? On gettin' all that much?"

"Naw. Shoot, I don't think the man knows what he's talkin' about," Jed said hurriedly. "Quarter, maybe . . ." And when he decided even that sounded cocky, he added, "ten cents. . . ."

Big Tate took off his shirt. "You go pump now," he said.

Jed stood at the kitchen sink pumping, watching his father's big shoulders. If he made money on his carvings, would his father like it or not? Talking to his father, Jed decided, was like standing out in the backyard and yelling at the mountain. Nothing ever seemed to get said —not really.

The day of the opening, there was mist in the morning, but by noon, the grass was dry and the sun was out. There were no church services this Sunday, so the people spent the morning putting the finishing touches on their wares and helping set up benches from the church basement outside Parsons' where the beer and cheese and soft drinks would be sold.

Beatrice put on a new pink dress that her mother had made for her, walking like a duck, Jed decided, swaying from side to side, heavy with the baby. She and Preston walked up the hill to the gathering, hand in hand, like school kids on a lark, glad for a change from the daily tedium and the preparations for a child that was coming all too soon.

Mrs. Tate was dressed up, too, with a red belt around her dark blue dress, and April Ruth had on a fancy pair of long green stockings that made her look like a flower on two long green stems.

Big Tate was in a good mood. He was looking forward to the cheese and beer, to sitting in the shade with the other men and making talk about how Tin Creek was finally going places. He was even prepared to forget Sedge Miles for one day. It was a time—one of the few—to be merry.

The Parsonses were there with loads of pickles and jams which they stacked on a table outside their store. April and her mother hung up the hooked rug on a line stretched across the

191

street between Parsons' and the crafts store, and Mrs. Tate even smiled at Mrs. Miles who was hanging up a rug beside Bea's.

"Nice day for the openin', ain't it?" Mrs. Tate ventured.

"Couldn't have ordered better," said Mrs. Miles.

It was a day for healing grudges.

Jed's four carvings—the fiddler, the pig, the hay wagon, and the goat—were on a small table at one side of the crafts store, in a space all by themselves. A hand-lettered sign said, "Hand-carved by Jed Jefferson Tate, aged 11." Jed couldn't bring himself to leave. He stood to one side, glancing over his shoulder at the little table, awed at seeing his own things there for sale along with the fine rockers and tables and belts made by the men.

"C'mon, Jed," Tommy yelled, running by. "Two cars from Morgantown just pulled up, and Mrs. Parsons said we could open a cracker barrel and pass 'em out free."

Jed ran after Tommy, and Jolly joined them. They filled their pockets with the small white crackers before they rolled the big barrel across the street.

There weren't a hundred cars that came. There weren't even fifty. But by four o'clock, when the crowd was at its peak, Jed counted twenty-one cars that didn't belong to Tin Creek people, and Tommy said there were two he'd missed. At first it seemed to Jed that no one was buying anything, but then he noticed that they liked to tour the whole store first and the street besides, stopping to taste the cheese and beer, before going back over the store again and picking out items they wanted to buy.

Five times Jed checked the little table where his carvings sat. Each time somebody seemed to be looking at them, but it wasn't until the fourth time he checked that he noticed two of his carvings were gone—the fiddler and the pig. He raced madly to Uncle Caully at the back of the store who was tending the money box.

"Uncle Caully!" he gasped. "Did they . . . ?"

Uncle Caully reached into the money box and held up four dollars and fifty cents. "Fiddler went for three-fifty and the pig for one," he said, grinning. "And seventy-five percent of it's yours, Jed."

Jed went over to a corner and closed his eyes tight, figuring. Seventy-five percent of four dollars fifty cents . . . He couldn't think. Three dollars? No . . . two? He closed his eyes even tighter and drew imaginary numbers in the air.

"Three dollars and thirty-eight cents," Uncle Caully said, grinning, and Jed's heart leaped. Wouldn't Ma be able to do something with that, though!

By five o'clock the hay wagon had been sold, too, for three dollars more. Only the goat remained, and Jed decided he'd been in too much of a hurry on that one. He'd have to go slower. He'd have to be sure that each piece was just as good as he could possibly make it.

A few more cars drove in at five-thirty, but by six o'clock, most of the tourists had gone, the shelves in the crafts store were half empty, and the tension was off. It had been a fairly good day. All of the baked goods and preserves had been sold, some of the rugs and rockers, and only a few quilts and cane-backed chairs remained. Uncle Caully and Mr. Parsons had gone off to count the proceeds. Then someone announced that the rest of the beer and soda was free, and there was much laughter and talk. The profits wouldn't bring more than a few dollars to each household. They wouldn't buy more than some extra meat and a pair or two of shoes. But that was better than nothing. And it might save the postal station and Aunt Etta's job if enough orders came in from out of state.

Big Tate liked his beer and so did Sedge Miles. Since two o'clock they'd been putting away pint after pint, and their talk and laughter

194

grew louder and louder. But nobody cared. Everyone was filled with the mood of the day and relaxed happily on scattered benches. Nobody cared, that is, until Sedge Miles, with another can of beer, walked over to the table where Big Tate sat with Mose Hardy and squinted at him curiously.

" 'At'sa guy!" he said drunkenly, holding his can carelessly while the foam ran down his arm. " 'At'sa guy whose kid pert' near drowned my Tommy out on the creek. . . ."

"Hush, Sedge," said his wife. "The flood's long since past. Don't dig for trouble."

But Sedge liked to talk, particularly when he got a reaction.

"Yep. 'At'sa guy, all right. Woulda knowed him anywhere. Ears are a little yellow around the edges. . . ."

Big Tate turned gropingly about and looked up at Sedge. "Go 'ang yourself," he muttered, and returned to his beer.

Sedge ignored him. "G'wan, admit it. You come from a long line of chicken fat, Tate, an' that's why you ain't keen on the strike, ain't it? Why, take that kid of yours—he can't swim, can't fight, and God 'elp 'im if he ever goes to the mines."

"You shut up, Sedge," Big Tate said, setting his beer down and spitting out of the cor-

ner of his mouth like an angry bull facing its
attacker. "Your boy can't swim no more'n he
can fly, an' it's only luck Jed was there to
save 'im."

Jed and Tommy, standing over by the
cracker barrel, felt suddenly on display and
looked quickly around for a way to get out, as
though that might somehow stop the argument.
But people were crowded around them on both
sides.

Sedge wasn't about to shut up. Beer made
some people drowsy, but it only made Tommy's father quarrelsome, and suddenly he
longed to say a few choice words to his long-
time enemy.

"You think everybody don't know it—
'bout the way the Tates got to be chicken?"
Sedge went on, leaning forward with one big
hand on his belly. "Why now, it goes back to
your grandfather, don't it—old chicken-livered
Grandpa Tate—who'd as soon leave a man dyin'
in the mines as a cat in a alley 'fore he'd risk
his own neck to save 'im—ain't that right,
Tate?"

Jed closed his eyes. Don't pay him no
mind, Pa, he whispered to himself. Don't pay
him no mind at all. Just go back to your beer
and look the other way. Just pick up the can
and go talk to Uncle Caully. Just . . .

196

A few choice words was all Sedge had in mind—just enough to get Jed's father riled up a little. But Big Tate sprang.

It was so quick that it took everyone by surprise. Jed hadn't known his father could move so fast, especially on a belly full of beer. There was a blue blur of Sam Tate's shirt as he lunged across the table, knocking bottles and cans to the ground, his big hands in a death grip around Sedge's neck.

"Pa," screamed Jed, but in an instant the two men, like savage bears, were rolling over and over in the middle of the street.

"You damned dog!" Big Tate was grunting, the words exploding from his lips. "You dirty—damned—dog!" He pulled back one fist and thrust it into one side of Sedge's nose, making it pour blood, and Tommy yelped. Sedge punched back, sending Big Tate sprawling, but each of them had more beer than most of the men in town could tolerate, and both were shaky on their legs. Sedge scrambled up and started to jump Big Tate while he was down, but fell over his own feet instead, giving Mr. Parsons and Mose Hardy a chance to move in and separate them.

Big Tate got up on one knee, one side of his face scraped raw from the fall. "You dirty, damned dog!" he screamed at Sedge who was being dragged away backwards. "The worst man was left in the mine! You know that!"

Big Tate's speech was followed by a string of curses between the men, and suddenly Jed's father was pulled into the back seat of Preston's car, and the car started downhill toward home, the back door swinging wide open.

Jed wanted to throw up. He wanted to rid himself of the awful scene that ruined the best day Tin Creek had ever seen. Tommy had left, and was walking along behind his own father, helping him stand up.

Jed felt horribly alone—alone and humiliated. He stood there by himself, looking around for Bea or April or any of his own kin to walk home with, but they had all disappeared. And then he saw Miss Singer looking at him from across the road. She had seen it all.

He turned and raced back behind Parsons' store, sloshed across the creek, and ran into the woods on the other side, running and running as though a hideous something was following him that he couldn't shake off.

He ran until he came to the foot of the mountain, where the black rock rose up beyond the pines and the grass tried to grow in scrubby patches on little ledges. Down beneath the mountain ran the seam of coal and the tunnels, some of them blocked years ago with rock and holding the bodies of men who never came up again.

Jed sat down, panting, in the spring dampness of the thick undergrowth and tried to remember the day as it had been up to that point. If only he hadn't seen it. If only he and Tommy had gone on home before it happened. If only he'd been somewhere else, and maybe just heard about it later, after it was all over, maybe somehow it wouldn't have seemed so awful.

But everyone had seen it. Everyone had heard. Everyone knew that Jed's father had lived so long underground that he couldn't think of anything else to do but pounce when things got too much for him.

He thought of running away, but he knew he wouldn't even get as far as Preston and Bea. You had to be sixteen to get a regular job, and even if he was, what could he do? Split wood? He was only fair at that. Slop pigs and feed chickens? Work the pump handle and hoe and dig potatoes? Those weren't the kinds of jobs you did in the city. And he didn't even have any kin in Morgantown to run off to.

Somehow he thought that if he stayed there in the woods long enough he'd think of something. It often worked that way. When the door stuck or the pump handle jammed or he'd carved too far in on one side of the hay wagon, Jed just put his mind to it for a while and thought hard and pretty soon he had a new way of looking at it and was usually able to fix it.

He was there by the mountain for almost three hours. But it didn't do any good. He couldn't leave Tin Creek, and he couldn't get the creek water out of his father's blood. What good did it do to bring tourists to the village if Big Tate and Sedge were going to turn it into a zoo? No matter how he tried to get away, no matter how he tried to make his life a little different, he'd end up same as Uncle Caully, with lungs full of coal dust or a leg gone or a back broken, and maybe a two-room house of his own to show for it when he was sixty-five.

He felt no better when he finally got up and started home. He was tired—dead tired—and all he wanted to do was lie face down on the cot in the front room and sleep.

His clothes were wet with the dampness of the woods, and his trousers were covered with burrs. He crossed the bridge and walked slowly up the hill toward home. He was half-way across his backyard when someone rose up from the bench and loomed tall against the night sky.

"Jed?"

It was his father.

"Yeah?"

For a moment there was silence. Then, "Where you been?"

"Off."

"Doin' what?"

"Thinkin', is all."

"Why didn't you tell your ma where you was at? You been gone a hell of a long time."

The anger at the bottom of Jed's stomach began to churn up again. "Figured she'd have 'er hands full with you. Wouldn't nobody miss me."

Big Tate spat out into the darkness. "What's that supposed to mean? You figure I was drunk?"

"Didn't have to figure on it. Anybody could see."

"I didn't have so much beer in me I couldn't tell an insult when I heard one," Big Tate said gruffly. "What'd you think I'd do? Sit there and let 'im smear me up and down the street—me and you and the whole Tate family?"

"Wouldn't everybody have fought it," Jed retorted. "Wouldn't everybody have to act like a animal and go tearin' a body limb from limb."

"That's certain!" The anger was rising in

201

his father's throat too. *"You* wouldn't. You'd let a body knock you down and walk on yer face and you'd still lie there. That's the kind of son I got. 'Fraid to scratch his big white hands."

The fury in Jed's chest blinded him. "What do you know about hands?" he choked. "You got paws, that's what. All you know is tearin' away at the coal and bustin' noses. You ain't got an eye for anything soft or pretty. You ain't never raised your eyes up further'n the top of the mountain. You don't even know there's a sky!"

It was more than Big Tate could take. A huge arm reached out and grabbed Jed's, the fingers closing around it as though it were a mere twig.

"You shut your mouth, boy. I'll not be listenin' to that kind of talk." The fingers gripped harder on Jed's arm and for a moment Jed wondered whether his father would break it. The big hand shook him violently, back and forth, back and forth, until Jed's teeth chattered, and then suddenly the hand let him go and Jed spun backwards, almost falling.

"One son I got," Big Tate said between clenched teeth, stepping forward. "One son I got, and I don't even know 'im."

In the darkness they stood there, facing each other, the red place on Jed's arm still stinging. Not another word was said, but the air was heavy with the hate between them. Finally, afraid to say more, Jed turned and walked into the house. He lay down on the cot in the front room, his arms hanging over the sides, feeling the pounding of his heart. In a few minutes, his father came in and sat down in the rocker. But he didn't pick up the newspaper. Jed lay there, his eyes closed, wondering when his father would say something.

"Jed . . . ?" his father said finally, softly. But Jed didn't answer. And figuring his son was asleep, Big Tate said nothing more.

There was very little talk in the Tate home the next few days. Jed came to the table as soon as he was called for meals, ate a bit, and left before the meal was over. When Big Tate came home from the mines, he came around the corner of the house without a word and waited till Jed got up and started the pump. There were times Jed caught his father looking at him, his eyes in a fixed, quizzical expression—worried, even, like he wanted to talk and didn't know how to begin. But Jed didn't care. He didn't talk to his father or give him a chance to talk to him, leaving the room as soon as he entered or sitting for long periods on the front porch or back stoop.

At school, a wall seemed to have sprung up

between Jed and Tommy, too. It was nothing that was said or done—only something felt—a distance between them that hadn't been there before, as though they each knew that this was the way it had to be, and it was useless to fight it any longer.

Miss Singer said nothing to either of the boys about what had happened. She knew the rules now—about questions that didn't concern her. Jed appreciated her silence, but it didn't help.

It was ten minutes before three on Thursday afternoon. Miss Singer was explaining a division problem to a small group of pupils at her desk. The younger children on the right side of the room were getting noisy, and everyone was anxious for school to let out. It was a warm day, a prelude to summer, and everything was tending to slow down, even Miss Singer's voice, which sounded tired.

All at once, as though to shock the warm May day out of its serenity, a whistle—loud and shrilly metallic—came ripping and cutting through the air—a wailing whistle like a thousand women screaming. Miss Singer was startled and looked around quickly for an explanation.

But Jed needed no second calling. With a half yell, he leaped up out of his seat, his knee banging his desk, his books skidding across the floor. He bounded out the door with Tommy, white-faced, behind him and a dozen children running along.

Like a thing gone mad, Jed skimmed the road in his bare feet, his tears choked up inside him as the whistle went on and on, never stopping, growing louder and louder in his ears. Still he ran, on up the hill beyond the schoolhouse, up, up along the dirt road, never stopping until he came to the entrance of the mine.

Chapter Twelve

All the while Jed was running on top of the ground, he thought about his father underneath. Was Big Tate running too? Was he trapped somewhere in the tunnel? Was he thinking about Jed the way Jed was thinking about him? Jed's heart thumped violently with the fear that was building up inside him.

Just as he reached the place where the fence began, the whistle stopped. It would not have to blow again. Everyone in Tin Creek and the surrounding villages knew what it meant. Trouble in the mine. Big trouble.

All his life, practically, Big Tate had worked the seam, and there hadn't been any great trouble. All the while that Jed and his father were getting along passably well, the disaster whistle had never sounded. But now, when they were hating each other so bitterly . . .

He thought about what Big Tate had said to his mother last Christmas—about not remembering the cross words if there should be a quarrel between them, but remembering *all* the things there were about a person, with quarreling only a part. Did that go for Jed, too?

Crowds of women were coming up the dirt road behind him on their way to the gate. Two were crying and holding onto each other. A company car went tearing by them on the edge of the road, and a man got out and ran through the fence ahead.

"My God, what is it? What is it?" cried Mrs. Parsons, catching up with Jed.

"A fire," another woman said, and the answer went traveling from woman to woman. "A fire . . . fire . . . fire . . . !"

At that very moment, there was a roar from the bowels of the earth, like thunder breaking loose beneath them. The ground shook and rumbled and suddenly, with a deafening boom, the cage shot right up out of the shaft like an artillery shell as flames and smoke spouted hundreds of feet into the air. Jed was knocked flat on his back, the force of the wind pressing him hard against the earth as a shower of cinders and rock came pelting down upon him and a piece of the shaft house flew by.

Women shrieked as they picked themselves up and rushed wildly back down the hill. Jed could see nothing inside the fence now except black billowing smoke. Cinders and other debris were still falling from the sky. Coughing and choking, he flung himself onto the road again and rolled downhill.

He came to rest against the trunk of a tree, his face in the dirt and his hands on the back of his neck. Like a dead man he lay, listening . . . waiting. The silence, after the explosion, was almost as terrifying as the roar. Not even a bird called from the grove of trees separating the mine from the meadow. No one stirred or whispered. Silence. Nothing.

And then a cricket chirped . . . a lone, questioning chirp, and chirped again. Slowly Jed raised his head and looked around. Women were clustered in groups all over the road, their arms about each other, their heads down. The sky was deep yellow-gray as the clouds of smoke spread wider and wider. Jed raised himself up on one elbow and looked up the hill toward the mine.

Inside the fence now, he could see men running. The shaft house was gone. The company car which had stood by the gate was overturned. One entire side of the tipple was gone, and wreckage was strewn all about the low roofs of the fan shed and the lamp house.

Two men came out to the road and began roping it off, urging the women to leave. A black dog, one of the miner's pets, howled forlornly, and slunk gingerly about, sniffing the smoke.

"Our men! Our men!" a woman began screaming.

"Nobody's comin' up out of this shaft, lady," a man told her. "Maybe the south portal —they might make it up there."

"Oh, Jed! Oh, Jed!" Mrs. Parsons wept, hugging him to her as though his pa were already dead, and Jed let the tears leak out for a moment, snuffing them back again as a truck came roaring out of the gate of the mine and took off across the meadow.

"They're goin' to the south portal!" someone cried, and everyone began to run after the truck, as again the earth rumbled and the gray smoke continued to pour out of the gaping hole where the shaft had stood.

Jed was at the end of the crowd now, as those farthest down the road led the way across the meadow. Another rescue truck came tearing out of the gate; it, too, taking the shortcut to the south portal.

In the crowd, Jed saw his mother and Bea up ahead. When he reached them, his mother grabbed his hand, hardly even looking at him, and rushed on, her face the color of chalk.

But after running most of the mile to the south portal, the news there was no better. The fire had burned right up through the shaft here, too, and the hoist man at the top, his face and arms burned, told how the cage lay in a charred and twisted heap at the bottom of the sump pit. And then he started to cry, and they drove him away in an ambulance.

A wail went up from the women, a deep, prolonged, paralyzing moan that seemed to electrify the air round them as they realized that the men were cut off from both portals. Their chances of reaching other escape routes, several miles away, grew slimmer and slimmer with each passing minute. Soon the whole vast underground maze would be a blazing inferno, and the only way to put out the fire would be to seal up the mine with concrete, the men inside it.

A group of girls from the junior high

school came running across the field, April Ruth among them. Her long hair tossed wildly about her head, and she still carried a load of school books.

"Ma!" she sobbed, flinging her books on the ground and falling into her mother's arms.

Lona Tate bit her lip and tried to comfort her. "We don't know nothin' yet, Ruthie. Nothin' at all."

A jeep came bouncing over the field, and this time there was a bit of hope. The driver said that most of the men had miraculously been assigned to the west tunnels that morning, nine miles away, and that they were bringing all the miners up through a portal in the next town. Only a few slushermen had been left behind in the south tunnel, perhaps nine or ten. The company officials were gathering at Parsons' store and had a list of the men who were working the south tunnel. If the women would just go there, they'd find out all they wanted to know.

Hope was the thing which had kept Tin Creek alive. Hope was the thing that sent the miners back into the earth every morning, that made it possible for their wives to plan for Christmas, and their children to count on shoes for school. Hope was the thing that made pinto beans taste good even when they weren't, because you hoped that after next pay day there might be a little bacon to cook with them. And so it was hope that started the women and children down the hill again, over the meadow, past the school, and on into town where the road outside Parsons' was swarming with cars of coal mine and union officials and reporters and photographers.

"Look at me, kid," said a photographer as Jed opened the screen at Parsons', noting his tear-stained cheeks. "You got a dad in the mines?" He held his camera up, waiting for Jed to turn.

"Get away from me," said Jed, almost inaudibly. "Just get *away*." The camera clicked anyway and Jed pushed on in beside his mother.

Mr. Parsons stood at the counter, leaning his weight on his hands, his head bent down as he listened for word of his oldest son. People sat on feed sacks and boxes, their faces taut, waiting for the company man in the gray suit by the door to read off the names of the men who had been working the south tunnel.

"This isn't like the old days," the man was saying. "This isn't like Monongah where they didn't even know how many men were down in the mine when the explosion went off. We're telling you everything we hear first we hear it. I'll not hold anything back . . ."

"Get on with it, then," a man from the union cried impatiently.

The man in the gray suit ignored the interruption. "There's been three explosions so far, all of them in the south tunnels close to the main shaft. We don't know what caused them or what damage they've done, but it doesn't look good, I'll tell you that. Four men were killed up on the ground by the main shaft when the explosion blew. Names were Charlie Voist, Ed Whittley, Chud Evers, and Daw Green."

"Lord, not Daw!" the women exclaimed, and relatives at the far end of the store began to sob.

The man in the gray suit waited, his face pained at the task before him. "Maybe you heard already that most of the men were working the west tunnels today, except for nine slushermen back in the south end. I can't guarantee that the men whose names I'm not reading are safe. We'll see as soon as they get up and over here. And I'm not saying that the men I'm gonna read are dead. It just looks the worst for them, that's all."

Jed sat motionless on a feed sack beside his mother and Bea, his chest so tight that he felt he couldn't breathe. Across the aisle stood Tommy Miles with his mother. Sarah Miles stood with her arms around Tommy, crossed in front of his chest. Jed and Tommy looked dully

213

at each other, scarcely recognizing the other. It was a time to be alone with one's own tears. Somehow Tommy looked miles and miles away, and Jed had the strange feeling that even if he called out, Tommy wouldn't hear him.

The man was unfolding a sheet of paper, the list of names.

Pa won't be on it, Jed promised himself wildly. He won't be on it, not out of a hundred or more men. He just won't. He waited, terrified.

"Easter Bingham," said the man. Another cry came from the back of the room.

"Bob Murphy, Dewey Messer, Lester Sizemore . . ."

"An' Lester too," a plaintive voice said.

"Mose Hardy . . ."

Bea gasped, and Aunt Etta reached down and embraced her, her eyes shut tightly.

"Jim Bromus, Sedge Miles . . ."

"No, no!" shrieked Tommy's mother, and someone led her outside.

"John Cromley and Samuel Tate."

A cry came from somewhere down in Lona's chest, a strange animal cry like one of pain and terror mixed. Aunt Etta let go of Bea and grabbed Lona in her arms, holding her close and rocking her back and forth.

The Parsons boy had not been called. Bea's

husband had not been called. But Jed couldn't think about that now. He didn't move. He sat motionless on the feed sack, his eyes large and unblinking, staring into Tommy's, neither boy seeing the other.

"Now I'm not saying these men are dead," the man in the gray suit said again. "There are lots of places they could be holed up in the tunnels if they were far enough away from the explosion and had time to get themselves barricaded in. We're doing all we can to check them out, and first word I get, you folks right here will know it."

Jed got up and went outside, struggling to breathe. The sun was just getting low in the sky, just beginning to turn the mountain into the gray-black giant that Jed knew so well. Any other afternoon Pa would be coming up about now. He'd be leaving his lamp at the lamphouse, and stopping a moment at the gate to talk with Mose or some of the other men. And then he'd come home, taking big giant steps down the road, past Parsons' and the little stores on the main street, around the bend, and then he'd be at the kitchen window whistling for Jed to turn on the water. But not today.

Cars kept coming, grinding up the dirt road and parking all over it. Women from the next town came bringing hot dishes to the church beyond the fork so that the waiting families would be fed. Reporters walked about with pencils and pads, asking questions about how much the men earned in the mines and how old they were when they started and how often their families had meat for supper. Jed wanted to punch them in the nose. He wanted to kick at their legs and make them go away. Instead, he went over to the church and stood around looking at the food spread on the table and thought about the mountain and his pa underneath. And when someone handed him a plate of spaghetti and applesauce, he shook his head and went outside again.

He stood there in the late afternoon shadows. Tin Creek had never been so crowded before. He had never seen so many cars at one time on the road in front of Parsons', not even for a family reunion. Even the Sizemores, with the biggest generation of all, never drew this many people.

Some reporters were standing on the grass outside the church, smoking and talking shop. Someone made a joke and the others laughed. Jed's stomach seemed to retch inside of him. That anyone could stand here and joke, when down below in the earth, his father . . . .

As his eye traveled up the bank to the road, he saw somebody else, somebody small and stooped over, sitting there under a tree. It was Tommy, and though Jed couldn't see his eyes in the shadows, the stoop of his shoulders told him how Tommy was feeling. Maybe he too knew what it was to feel two ways about somebody—to love and hate someone at the same time and miss him terribly when he was gone. At that moment Tommy looked down at him and Jed felt a tremendous urge to go talk to Tommy. But just as he started forward, a car came careening around the corner and swerved to a stop.

A man jumped out and ran over to the reporters gathered there on the grass. In thirty seconds, the news was traveling all through the church where the people were eating, across the road to Parsons', and people began pouring outside and running back up the hill to the schoolhouse and on beyond to the mine, Jed running with them.

The rescue teams had heard a banging noise coming from one end of the big air shafts three-quarters of a mile away, the rumor went. It was possible that some of the men had clustered there at the foot of the 600-foot shaft, and that the rush of air down it was enough to keep back the fire and smoke—for a while, at least.

As quickly as possible, the rescue workers

were trying to rope off the area around the ventilator shaft. By the time Jed and the others reached it, trucks were positioned around it beaming huge lights toward the shaft. Already workmen were hammering away at the top to remove the head so that a bucket scoop could be lowered deep down into the ground.

The crowd understood the necessity for keeping back. At one point, one of the workmen took a crowbar and pounded three times on the top of the vent. All was silent except for the hum of the big trucks. And then, from deep below, came the sound: rap, rap, rap.

Frantically the workmen tore at the lid of the vent, until finally the head was off and a hoist was moved over the top with the bucket scoop in position.

"She's ready," a rescue worker said finally. As the machinery began to grind, a cable was loosened, and the bucket dropped into the shaft.

To Jed, it was an interminable wait. Bea and April Ruth were crying, and Mrs. Tate clasped Jed's hand so tightly that it hurt. He dripped with perspiration, and his large eyes were so fixed on the hoist over the hole that he felt he could not even blink them.

The scoop had reached bottom. Finally the cable turned the other way, and the bucket was coming up. The tension mounted as the scoop came closer and closer to the top. Finally a head emerged—two heads—and the first two miners, their faces black, were lifted from the scoop as the bucket went down again without a moment wasted.

Everyone surged forward, blocking Jed's view.

"Pa? Pa?" Jed called, but everyone else was calling too, and as the two exhausted miners were quickly hustled into the first aid truck, their names circulated through the crowd: Mose Hardy and Lester Sizemore.

The scoop was coming up again and Jed pressed his arm against his chest to stop the painful throbbing of his heart. But Big Tate wasn't on this load either. The waiting women cried out and tried to question the rescued miners about who else was waiting below in the blackness. But no one was sure. The explosion had happened so fast, the tension was so great, and the pit had been so black with smoke that they couldn't see. The miners had linked hands, coughing and vomiting from the acrid smoke, and made their way through the darkness to the air vent, where the air coming in from above and their own emergency inhalators prolonged their lives. Lester Sizemore had done the pounding, they said. It was his idea. But beyond that, all they knew for sure were the names of the men in their crew that morning. Who had made it to the air vent and who did not, they didn't know.

A truck arrived with rescued men from the west end. The Parsons boy and Preston were among them. Bea threw her arms around her husband's neck, and then Preston went on into the first aid truck to see his father.

Again the scoop was lowered and again it returned, this time with John Cromley and Easter Bingham.

Jed didn't think he could stand it. The tension of waiting tore at his stomach as the bucket went down again. He wanted to run over to the air vent and scream down his father's name, but the rescue workers pulled him back.

"You'd not be helpin', lad," he was told.

This time Jed recognized neither of the men who stepped out of the scoop. The grime was thick on their faces, showing only their teeth and the whites of their eyes. But Jed had to know—had to see. He broke away from the restraining arms of the workers and flung himself over to the miners, his eyes huge and terrified.

One of the men, the tallest, took a towel which someone handed him and began wiping the grime out of his eyes. Jed cried out with the anguish of not knowing, and the towel came down. And then he saw it was Big Tate, as black as midnight, his teeth gleaming white between his blackened lips.

"Pa . . ." Jed couldn't move. The relief was so great that it rushed over him like a warm shower, slowing his pounding heart and relaxing his stretched eyelids. "Pa . . ." he said again, barely audible, unable to move.

For a moment the big black man stared at his son, the tears making white rivulets on his grimy cheeks, and in that moment, they seemed to say a hundred things they could never tell each other aloud.

"Hello, Jed," said Big Tate, and he was smiling. "It's okay now."

"Yeah," said Jed. "It's okay." He gulped and tried to say more, but he couldn't. Big Tate reached over and squeezed his shoulder with one big hand.

And then Lona was there, kissing her husband and getting grime all over her dress and cheeks and arms, but she didn't care.

When the scoop bucket went down a fifth time, it came up empty.

"Nobody else down there?" the rescue workers asked the miners who were gathering around the opening.

"Who's up?" asked Mose Hardy from the stretcher where he lay resting, exhaustion in his voice.

The crowd called out the names of the men who had come up.

Big Tate dropped his arms from around Lona's shoulder and swung around. "Sedge Miles? Anybody seen Sedge?"

"He didn't come up," somebody answered. "He weren't one of 'em."

Big Tate's head darted to the left and then to the right, seeking the answer. "Sedge," he said loudly. "Where's Sedge?"

"He didn't come up, Sam," the people insisted.

"He was behind me," Big Tate insisted. "I heard him. I know that voice. It was Sedge, all right."

"You sure now, Sam?" asked Lester Size-more. "Easy to make a mistake, you know. Sure it wasn't one of us?"

"It was Sedge," said Jed's father, and the way he said it, no one questioned. "He was be-hind me when we were feelin' our way to the vent. He was with us then."

There was a sob from the crowd and Tom-my's mother turned her face away.

Jed looked around. Tommy was standing there behind him, his face white, his lips half open, but not moving. At that moment the ground shook with the force of another explosion. In the distance, the smoke billowed again from the main shaft, rising hundreds of feet into the air, and some began wafting up from the air vent itself.

"He didn't make it to the vent, he won't make it at all," said one of the rescue workers, trying to push the crowd back lest the vent explode also. "It's an inferno down there. The last time the scoop came up, it was hot."

Big Tate grabbed at a breathing apparatus. "Give me a McCaa," he said. "I'm goin' down to git Sedge."

"You're crazy," said someone. "A McCaa ain't goin' to keep you from burnin' to death. Look at that smoke. If Miles was anywhere near the vent he'd have made it. Nobody can go down there till it cools off."

"I'm goin' to get Sedge," Big Tate repeated, climbing into the scoop. "He's somewhere close. I know it."

"Sam...!" said Lona, and then she stopped and let him go. Jed knew that trying to stop Big Tate was like trying to stop a storm from crossing the mountain—it was something he had to do.

Jed stood riveted to the ground, watching as his father's head disappeared, and felt that his stomach was sinking, too. Pa had been safe. For a moment they had him back again. Now he was going down where even the rescue crew wouldn't go, and all for Sedge Miles.

Lona did not weep. She put her arms around Tommy's mother, and they stood silently.

Tommy walked away from the crowd and sat down on the side of the hill, looking as though he were going to be sick. Jed followed and sat down, too, both of them staring at the air vent, neither of them talking.

Finally Tommy said, "He knowed it was goin' to happen. He talked about it every day almost. He'd say, 'They don't rock-dust this week, it's goin' to come.' Every day he'd say that. And finally it came."

"Pa'll find him," Jed said, not believing it. "Pa'll bring him up."

The minutes dragged on, and both pretended not to notice the smoke wafting up out of the vent. The circuit minister arrived. He knelt on the ground, and the women knelt around him, and all the other miners stood with their heads down, praying, too.

And suddenly, as Jed sat looking at Tommy, sitting there all stooped over, his arms around his knees, he remembered what he'd wanted to say to him outside the church.

224

"Tommy," he said quickly, his throat tight. "No matter who comes up or who don't, you and me can't go 'round not speakin'."

Tommy gulped. "Pa knew the Tates weren't chicken, Jed. He knew how it was out there on the river. I told him. But it was so long in him—that story that was told him about Grandpa—I reckon he just chose to believe it. Don't really matter no more whether it was true or not."

"But we got to stop it, Tommy. We got to decide on it now, before we know how it's gonna turn out. . . ."

Tommy stretched out his hand and they shook on it. He was making funny yipping noises in his throat, as though he were trying to stop the sobs which were forcing their way out. Jed wished he'd go ahead and cry. He didn't care. And finally Tommy did—soft jerky cries at first and then long, breathy cries from the bottom of his lungs. Finally it seemed he didn't have any tears left, and he grew quiet.

At that moment, there was a new roll of thunder below the earth, and then the ground shook with another blast. A wail went up from the women as black smoke billowed out of the vent itself, and the minister put his hands up to the sky and cried out, "Oh, God! Oh, God! Oh, God!"

And then, suddenly, the bucket was coming up—coming up in the smoke. Lona and Sarah Miles clasped each other tightly. Jed and Tommy sat side by side, frozen. The circuit minister was on his knees, praying silently, only his lips moving. The miners gathered around the hole, their hands extended—waiting. Had he done it? Had Big Tate rescued Sedge? Was he coming back alone? Or was it Sedge coming this time and Sam Harrison Tate who was left behind?

Never had the minutes moved more slowly. Finally the top of a man's head emerged, and again Jed could see nothing because of the miners who were gathered around. But then he heard a man yelling, "Give 'em room, give 'em room," and Big Tate stumbled out of the scoop, half carrying Sedge, their shirts ripped off their backs, their hair singed. A cheer went up, a spontaneous triumphant roar of man over mine.

"He's okay, Sarah," Big Tate said to Tommy's mother. "A timber had him pinned and he took a lot of smoke. But he's breathin' okay and he'll be all right. Don't you worry."

And even as the miners rushed the people away from the dangerous hole, pushing them back farther and farther away from the possibility of more explosions, Jed and Tommy were

226

rolling deliriously downhill, shrieking happily, making noontime out of the coming night.

It was a miracle, everyone said. It was the worst disaster Number 7 had ever seen, and it took the lives of four men up above. But not a miner below had lost his life. Old Mose Hardy, it was discovered later, had been injured more severely than he knew, and his lungs would never again take the mine. But that all the others were safe—that was a miracle worth telling again and again. Some said it was God and some said it was luck and some said it had something to do with Sam Tate being the brother-in-law of Etta, who was the seventh child of a seventh child and had a power nobody else could understand. Whatever it was, Jed knew that courage had a lot to do with it, and Tommy's father knew it, too.

Chapter Thirteen

The strike, of course, was off. Union officials and state and federal inspectors flocked over the area—probing the cause of the explosion and investigating safety conditions in the other mines as well. Number 7 was sealed with concrete and wouldn't be opened again for many months until the fires below had stopped burning. The area was still dangerous, and no one was allowed up by the main shaft. Gas was still escaping, and was even found bubbling up in the creek.

The men were given a week off at company

expense. It was a silent week in which those who were alive thrilled to the sense of waking each morning to a new day, and the relatives of those who had died prepared for the funerals.

Jed and his family went to the funeral of Daw Green, the brash young man who had entered the mine the day he left school, who prided himself on his strength and brawn and would have worked in no other place if given a chance, which, of course, he wasn't.

The circuit minister preached the service in the "big church"—the outdoor place way up on the hill, far beyond the church and the parsonage and bosses' row, where the wind blew all the time and the small graveyard bore the bodies of Tin Creek men who had died in the depths of the earth.

Jed sat motionless beside his father, his eyes wide. It was a place nobody ever went if he could help it. It was the place, for one thing, where young Daw Green had cut the ears off a live possum, and the strange little animal never even moved, just went on playing dead. Now it was said that if you came up here at night, you'd see the eyes of that ghost possum shining at you in the darkness. Jed wondered if it haunted Daw's grave.

It was a place, too, of Indian graves, and

everyone knew there were Indian spirits around the springs where the rocks were smoothed over in a mysterious way. It was also the spot in Tin Creek where berries grew best, and there were more snakes here than anywhere else. It was said that rattlesnakes sat in the bushes, and you couldn't even hear them singing. One woman was killed up here at berry picking time by rattlesnakes, the story went, and when they found her body there were forty snakes on it. All this went through Jed's mind as he sat close to his father, watching the minister praying, and listening to the rush of wind in the big trees overhead.

When the praying was over, Daw Green was buried beneath a stone that said, "Asleep in Jesus," and the people went home.

"It's borrowed time, that's what we've got," Lona sobbed as she leaned on Big Tate's arm. "We've none of us got any notion how soon it's goin' to happen again—how soon the mine's goin' to take another one."

Big Tate could not find the words to comfort her, but Uncle Caully, hobbling along beside, felt differently. "You watch and see, Lona. Once them inspectors git through, there ain't goin' to be a lot of dust left. Once a happening like this takes place, they got to see that it don't happen again. It's been in all the newspapers. Everyone's watchin'."

"There ain't no guarantees, Caully," Lona said, wiping her eyes.

"No, nor about nothin' else neither. But you can be sure the mine Sam's goin' back to is gonna be safer than the one he left."

When the week had passed, the miners of Tin Creek were picked up each morning in trucks and taken to Number 8, fifteen miles away, till their own seam could be worked once more. Slowly, life settled back into the usual routine as the month of May wore on. The sky turned bluer and the air was warmer, the children went to school without their shoes, and the villagers made ready each week for the tourists who drove up the winding dirt road on weekends.

But it was the mail orders that fanned Aunt Etta's hope that Tin Creek Crafts would be a success. Each week the orders slowly increased, and there was a waiting list for the most popular items. But Etta was a realist. She said it might turn out that interest in homemade things wouldn't last. But as long as there were even four or five cars on a Sunday afternoon, and enough orders during the week to keep the postal station alive, the people felt it was worth it, for it strengthened their sense of community spirit.

Everybody talked about Big Tate. Everyone said that if anybody could have found

Sedge slumped back there in the tunnel where the timbers had fallen, it was Sam. And when Jed and his father walked up the road to Parsons' to buy a cigar or across the street to the nickel-and-dime, everybody said, "How ya' doin', Sam?" "Nice goin', Tate." "Good to see ya." As Jed looked up at his father, the man seemed a lot taller than Jed had ever noticed, like he had to throw back his head almost to see the top of Pa's. Maybe it was just that he'd never walked so close to his pa before. It was a good feeling. It was nice to have a hero in the family, even if it was the kind of hero you might never be yourself.

Jed had begun some new carvings, and his mother was continually amazed.

"Can't figure it," she said at the breakfast table one morning. "Jed picks up an old hunk of pine in the backyard, makes somethin' of it, and folks pay part of a week's groceries to carry it home."

Big Tate spread his bread heavily with apple butter. "It's not the wood they're payin' for, it's the work. Looks simple enough, I guess, but when it comes to makin' one yourself. . . ." He smiled and looked over at Jed. "What you gonna do with all that money, Jed?"

"He already give me half for food money," said Lona. "Isn't that just like him, though?"

"He's givin' it away?" said Big Tate. "Jed, it's yours, you know—to do with as you want."

"Oh, I'm keepin' some," said Jed. "I got six dollars put away. I got a plan for it."

April Ruth was strangely restless. The village seemed to be moving and passing her by. The hooked rugs she was making with Bea were boring, and the work she'd done on the last one was so sloppy that Aunt Etta sent it back again to do over. It wasn't what April wanted to do at all. Jed seemed to understand, even though they'd never talked about it. He knew what she was feeling and why.

"Jed," said Miss Singer at recess one afternoon. "Could you stay a few minutes? I won't keep you long."

Now what, Jed wondered. Was his science paper all that bad? Did she find out that he'd copied the migration of birds right out of the minister's encyclopedia? But Miss Singer wasn't talking about birds.

"Jed," she said, and her eyes sparkled excitedly. "I've got some wonderful news, if you're interested. If you won't think I'm . . . pushing . . ."

Pushing what? "No, ma'am," Jed said.

"Every teacher in the county gets to choose one pupil to take a special course in Morgantown this summer. It's a government project to train young people in different fields. You're a little young, but I read about a course in woodworking that I think might interest you. They teach all kinds of things—starting with your own special skills and interests—wood carving, sculpture, cabinetmaking, chair mending, ornamental work, finishing—everything that has to do with wood. It wouldn't cost anything except your transportation to Morgantown twice a week for ten weeks. Do you think you would . . . do you want to go?"

She waited, holding her breath. She was trying not to push, not to pry.

"I could—maybe—get me a job later on? Be a cabinetmaker or carve table legs or things like that?"

"Exactly. That's it. It would be a specialty, and I'm sure it would open up all kinds of doors for you. But . . ." she paused. "Of course, it's up to you."

Jed stood still, trying to calculate the round-trip bus fare to Morgantown, twice a week for ten weeks.

"Bus fare comes to thirteen dollars," Miss Singer said, reading his mind. "I know that's a lot of money. But you're earning some with your carvings, and I thought . . ."

234

"I can't," said Jed, his heart sinking. "I guess I can't."

"Because of the money?"

He nodded.

"You haven't earned that much? You don't think you could earn that much by the middle of June?"

"No . . . I'll have enough, but . . . I was savin' it for somethin' else," Jed said. And then, because she didn't ask, he told her. "A piano."

"A *piano*, Jed?"

"Not for me. For my sister. For April."

"Any . . . special kind of piano?"

"No. Just a piano. One that plays pretty good, is all."

Now Miss Singer was really excited. "Well, I just happen to know someone who's giving a piano away for the hauling. At least, she was last week. Of course, it's not a great piano, you understand—it's an old upright, and it's horribly scratched on one side, but it plays. She's a friend of mine in Grafton who teaches kindergarten, and she told me the school is getting a new one."

"I'll take it!" Jed yelped.

"But how will you get it here?"

"I don't know, but I'll do it. I'll get to Grafton this afternoon if she still has it."

Miss Singer looked at her watch. "There's fifteen minutes left of recess. I'll run over to the minister's house right now and phone."

She was back in ten. "She still has it, Jed, and I told her you'd come by this afternoon. She'll be there till four-thirty." Miss Singer wrote down the name and address and gave it to him, and Jed rushed out to the playground.

He skidded to a stop in the dust and grabbed Tommy by the shirt. "You got to help me get a piano," he gasped. "I got to get it this afternoon. I'm goin' to ask Aunt Etta to drive me to Grafton, and you come, too, and help push."

"How you goin' to get a piano? Steal it?" Tommy asked, unbelieving.

"It's for free! It's for April Ruth, and you got to be quiet about it."

"I'll go too," said Jolly. "I'll get my brother and we'll all push."

Good old Jolly. Whenever Jed needed her, she was there—always willing to help. And what did she get in return? Buckeyes thrown at her knees. Teasing. Poking.

"Jolly, you aren't hardly like a girl at all. You're a real sport," Jed told her appreciatively.

She was, too. If she had a dream of her own, she never mentioned it, except to belong to God and go to heaven when she died. Maybe that's what she was working on. Maybe that's why she was always ready to help somebody else. Perhaps he'd carve something for Jolly at the woodworking class—a bracelet, maybe. He'd keep it in mind.

Miss Singer let the three off school early, and Jolly stopped at the store to get one of her older brothers who was stacking soup cans. As they passed the Tates' house, Jed stuck his head in the door long enough to yell, "I'm going to Aunt Etta's, Ma," and ran on down the hill with his friends behind him.

Aunt Etta was soaking a corn on her foot, with her other leg propped up on a chair and a Sears catalog in her lap.

Jed swung himself onto the porch beside her. "Aunt Etta, would you do anythin' in the world for me if I asked?"

Aunt Etta slowly closed the catalog. "Now, Jed . . ."

"If it were to do somebody a whole lot of good?"

Aunt Etta stared at the waiting faces on the grass. "I reckon, if I was able. What you thinkin' up now?"

"Aunt Etta, you just got to drive me to Grafton right now and pick up a piano."

Aunt Etta's foot slid off the chair and

landed in the bucket beside the other. "A piano! Jed Jefferson Tate, you got no mind at all? What for?"

"April Ruth."

"How you gonna buy a piano?"

"It's free."

"Where's it at?"

"A school, and they're waitin' for me. Miss Singer fixed it up. I got the address, but I got to get there before four-thirty."

Aunt Etta lifted her feet out of the bucket, pulled on her stockings, and felt around for her shoes. "I ain't gonna ask no more questions, 'cause if I think of any more I'll say no. Caully!" she called, "I'm off to Grafton, and if Lona asks, tell 'er Jed's with me? Hear?"

Uncle Caully came to the door with his mouth open, but before he could shout "What for?" the pickup truck was rolling on down the hill with four kids in the back, heading for the highway.

It was almost four when they reached the school in Grafton, and Miss Singer's friend was waiting for them.

"How are you going to get it in the truck?" she asked. "You'll damage it if you drop it. Do you have a roller?"

They had nothing but arms, and Aunt Etta sat in the truck with her head in hers, wondering how in the world she'd thought she could haul a piano.

Jolly and her big brother and Jed and Tommy went inside and got the piano as far as the door. There were three steps to get down, a hole in the sidewalk to get across, and then a four-foot climb to the back of the truck.

For another twenty minutes they searched the neighborhood and the school basement for planks, while Jed's aunt followed numbly, whispering promises to herself.

They found four thick boards which they used to make a ramp over the steps. Then, with the help of a telephone repairman who was passing by and the school janitor, they got the piano down the steps and across the hole in the sidewalk. Then they set the boards up the other way to push it into the truck, where it settled with a thump, and the back end of the small truck sagged low over the wheels.

Miss Singer's friend and the telephone repairman and the school janitor were as relieved as Aunt Etta, and Jed was still thanking the teacher from the back of the truck when Aunt Etta started down the hill for home, eager to be done with her part of the bargain.

Grafton was a town of many hills. On one side of the streets, the houses were perched far above the road, and on the other side, they were down below. Sometimes the sidewalks were simply stairs of concrete going up the side of a hill. The front yards were narrow, with big cement walls to hold the earth back. The river ran far down below, with railroad tracks beside it—no place for a tall piano in a low truck with a nervous driver and four jubilant children.

Every time the sagging pickup rounded a bend, the piano started to lean. Each time Aunt Etta went around a corner, the four children would clamber to the other side of the truck and wedge themselves between the low side of the truck and the piano to keep it from tipping. And each time Aunt Etta looked in her rearview mirror and saw the piano teetering precariously this way and that, and the four children—who were infinitely more precious— trying to hold it up, her eyes would close for a moment and her hands would grip the wheel hard, and she would promise anyone who was listening that if He would just give her her wits back, she would never lose them again.

Now, as they neared home, Jed's heart began to pound. What was Ma going to say when she saw it? Where in the world would they put it? It could go behind the stove in the front room if Jed moved his cot out on the back porch, but then it would mean sleeping out

240

there all winter. Still, there was just no other place. Maybe, by winter, Bea and Preston would be living with Mose Hardy, and April Ruth could move back into the small bedroom again and take the piano with her. That was it. That was the only thing to do.

April Ruth was sitting on the front steps when they came up the hill. She was barefoot and working on a little dress she was sewing for Bea's baby. She looked up when she heard the truck coming and squinted her eyes, trying to make out who and what was in it. Slowly her mouth dropped open and her eyes widened. And then, when she realized what it was, she screamed, "Ma! Ma!" And throwing the baby dress halfway over the grass, she leaped off the steps and flung herself across the yard.

She seemed to know it was for her, though why or how was completely beyond her understanding. She leaped onto the truck and wrapped her two skinny arms around the piano, grinning and laughing and moaning to herself, while Jolly's brother stared at her like she was a girl gone mad and backed down off the truck.

Mrs. Tate stood in the doorway, looking at the strange sight there in the street.

Aunt Etta got out and came around.

"I'm plumb out of my mind, Lona—the blame's on me," she said. "My head's gone soft to let Jed talk me into it, I swear."

"You mean, it's *ours?*" Mrs. Tate came down the steps. "Jed! How . . . ?"

"It's for April," said Jed. "We just got to keep it for her, Ma. It's sort of . . . uh . . . like a gift."

However Jed had come by the piano, it was clear to his mother that April Ruth could not possibly be separated from it. She clung to the old upright, one leg entwined around it, and Lona knew that if she tried to send it back, April would climb inside and close the lid.

"Where's it gonna go, Jed?" she asked getting no sense out of April, who was still moaning.

"I'm movin' my cot out on the back stoop," Jed explained. "The piano can go behind the stove in the front room. Then, when Bea and Preston move out, the piano can go into April's room with her."

"The mosquitos are thick as gravy on that back stoop," Lona said gently.

"They won't bother me none," Jed said. "Besides," he added, grinning, "April's playin' will drive 'em away."

There was something about music in the

house that didn't make it seem like Tin Creek anymore, even though it was the slow plank plunk of April's fingers. Somehow, of a Sunday, it made Jed feel good to sit out on the back stoop and work on his carvings and hear piano music coming from inside. It was like the homes in Morgantown where you could walk past and hear somebody practicing.

It helped them all forget, for a time, that Number 7 had maybe only a year left in it— that Pa and lots of other men would have to find work in another mine or go on welfare. Sometimes Sam even talked about picking up and moving to Tennessee, but you had to have money to move. You had to have a place to go to.

Music helped Bea forget that she'd soon be taking care of Mose Hardy as well as a new baby. It helped Jed and April Ruth forget that there was no place to go after high school for people without money, and it made Lona forget, for a while, the many fears she carried around inside her all the while her husband was working beneath the mountain.

"Now I got me a *home*," Big Tate would say. "Pretty soon I'll come home in the evenin's and hear Bea's baby cryin' and April Ruth's playin', and Sedge and me'll git together at the kitchen table for a game of gin, and it'll be like when Lona was young and the kids were small and we didn't worry so much."

"You won't be hearin' the baby long, Pa," Bea said, and she was happier somehow, because the family was happy. "Preston and me are movin' in with Mose come October."

"I get my first raise in July," said Preston.

"It's a good job, the mines," Big Tate said. "The money's good." He glanced at Jed, and then said quickly, " 'Course, there are other jobs good too. An' cabinet makin', I hear, pays real good in the cities."

"Jed was the only one in the whole school picked," Lona said proudly. "He'll do all right if he gets on furniture. Why, he'll be called for from Morgantown and Grafton and all places around. Once he gits himself known."

The days went by quickly. Miss Singer cleaned out cupboards and drawers and assigned various children odd jobs to help get ready for the closing of school.

"What would you say, Jed?" Miss Singer asked, smiling, "if I told you I was coming back next fall?"

Jed stopped wiping the blackboard. "I'd say you was jokin'."

She laughed out loud. "Well, I'm not joking. I am coming back. It took a long time, but I'm finally getting to feel as though I belong here—just a little. I'm not saying it will last, but I'd like to try it for another year at least."

Jed looked at her proudly. She didn't scare off so easy, Miss Singer. And Jed bet that when she ever did leave Tin Creek, there would be a lot of people that would miss her.

The twelfth of June came rapidly, and Jed had saved almost enough for his bus fare to Morgantown for ten weeks. There was considerable excitement around the breakfast table that morning, and even Bea got up in time to see Jed off. Uncle Caully and Aunt Etta came up the road bringing corn muffins and marmalade, and everyone sat around the big table in the kitchen at seven o'clock in the morning, having a party.

"Here's what you do, Jed," said Uncle Caully, stuffing half a muffin in his mouth. "First thing you do, when you get there, you find out which job pays the best—cabinet makin' or furniture repairin' or carvin' pretty things or what—and then that's what you study. Do that and you can't go wrong."

Big Tate laughed. "I don't know about that, Caully. I think Jed should figure it out for himself, and do the thing he really wants most."

"No matter what it is, it'll be good—somethin' he can do for a livin' here or any place else," said Preston, and it was sad the way he said it—like he'd give anything to have the chance that Jed had—a chance to get up out of the mine and do something under the sky again.

"Well, I don't know." Aunt Etta gestured with her spoon. "Jed always was a dreamer, and you can't go far on that . . ."

"But if you don't have no dreams, you won't go nowhere at all," April Ruth said, sticking up fiercely for her brother. "A dream's the startin' place of anythin' you're goin' to be." She was thoughtful a moment and toyed with the piece of fried mush on her plate. " 'Course, it may be you won't have the whole dream. It may be you have to learn to be happy with just a little piece of it comin' true. But gettin' part way is better'n not gettin' anywheres at all."

Bea turned heavily around in her chair. "I been sewin' on a new shirt for you, Jed, to wear your first day in Morgantown. But I still got the buttonholes to do. Maybe you can wear it next week."

"Lord, Bea, you ought to be workin' on baby clothes instead," Jed told her appreciatively.

Big Tate would be leaving soon and then Jed, so there was much scurrying about to get them both ready and their lunches packed.

246

"I put in a piece of chicken left over," Lona told Jed. "An' some buttered bread an' a raw turnip. An' just for extra . . ." She took a dime from her apron and gave it to him. "You can use this in one of them candy machines. Keep you from starvin' till suppertime." Suddenly she grabbed his face in her hands and kissed his forehead. "Jed, I'm *real* proud of you, *real* proud . . ."

Big Tate was out in the backyard lacing up his thick boots when Jed came out. His miner's cap was on sideways, with the light leaning over to one side.

"Pa, I finished another carvin' last night," Jed said. "Been workin' on this for a couple months."

"Sounds like somethin' special, Jed. Should sell first off on Sunday, I'll bet. . . ."

"I ain't gonna sell this one," Jed told him.

"Why not?"

"I made it for you." Jed held something out. "You know . . . to keep if you want."

Big Tate raised up and slowly lowered his boot to the ground. There, in Jed's hands, carved from a hunk of black coal, was the mountain— the big, hulk of a mountain—with the same lines and shapes and bulges that he saw every day when he stood on the back stoop of a morning and looked out beyond the woods. And yet, as

Jed turned the carving a little, a mountain slowly became something else right in front of Big Tate's eyes—became the profile of a man's head, bent, with a strong forehead and nose and a large cubed chin and a tuft of hair that stood out straight from the back of the neck the way Big Tate's did when he bent over the newspaper on the table.

Big Tate stared silently at the carving, reaching out and touching it with his fingers, and finally taking it in his own big hands and turning it around.

"I don't know where you came by this talent of yours, Jed—I really don't," he said finally. "A mountain was good enough, but . . ." He stared up at the mountain in the distance, looming beyond the backyard. "It does look like a man's head, don't it—if you look at it right?"

"I always thought it did," Jed grinned. "I always thought it looked like you, Pa. It's a . . . a strong-lookin' montain, ain't it?"

Big Tate smiled at Jed. "You got an eye for things like this, Jed, and it's a gift I don't understand. But I'm glad you got it. I really am."

Big Tate put on his other boot and stood up. "Set this in the kitchen window so's I can see it mornin's and evenin's," he said, putting the carving back in Jed's hands. "And maybe . . ." He smiled. "Maybe it'll remind me to look up at the sky now and then."

Big Tate picked up his old gray lunch bucket and started down the road to the junction where a truck picked up the miners and took them to Number 8. Jed watched him go. Taking the mountain in his hands, he went back inside.

Phyllis Reynolds Naylor has been writing since she was a teenager and has had children's novels, short story collections and picture books published.

She is very interested in social problems and enjoys music, drama, art, and travel.

Mrs. Naylor, her husband, and two young sons live in Bethesda, Maryland.

Also by Phyllis Reynolds Naylor

To Make A Wee Moon
Meet Murdock
Making It Happen